We scrambled . could, but we were too late. The sled, with Arnold barely holding on, was already a hundred yards down the road. The dogs ran at full speed, howling happily while Arnold bounced wildly on the rear runner.

We stood there for just a moment in shock. Then Fernando jumped on the KC Snow Tracker. He shouted to the rest of us in a take-charge voice . . .

"Curtis, Megan, you guys stay behind. Maybe the dogs'll come back when they're tired or hungry." He pointed to the seat behind him on the Snow Tracker. "Keisha . . . ? C'mon with me." Fernando gunned the engine and we burst forward, following the trail left by the dog sled.

Then, just as we whipped around a blind corner, I saw a dark shape step into the trail ahead of us. A moose!

There was no time to stop and nowhere else to steer. Unless we wanted to smack into a spruce tree instead, we were going to hit the side of that moose like a freight train.

⟾⬦⟽

**KINETIC
CITY**
super crew

**Other Books in
The Kinetic City
Super Crew Series**

Snow Problem

The Case of the Mushing Madness

Marianne Meyer

**LEARNING
TRIANGLE
PRESS**

*Connecting
kids, parents, and teachers
through learning*

An imprint of McGraw-Hill

New York San Francisco Washington, D.C. Auckland Bogotá Caracas
Lisbon London Madrid Mexico City Milan Montreal New Delhi
San Juan Singapore Sydney Tokyo Toronto

McGraw-Hill

*A Division of The **McGraw·Hill** Companies*

Library of Congress Cataloging-in-Publication Data applied for.

2 3 4 5 6 7 8 9 0 DOC/DOC 9 0 3 2 1 0 9 8

ISBN 0-07-006693-0

The sponsoring editor for this book was Judith Terrill-Breuer, the senior producer was Joe Shepherd, the editing supervisor was Jane Palmieri, and the production supervisor was Clare B. Stanley. It was set in Century Old Style by Dennis J. Smith of McGraw-Hill's Professional Book Group in Hightstown, New Jersey.

Printed and bound by R. R. Donnelley & Sons Company.

Contents

About the Crew

It is the near future. Peace has broken out all over the world, and the President of the United States has decided to donate the world's most sophisticated military vehicle, the X-100 Advanced Tactical Vehicle, to "the youth of America, that they might use this powerful tool to learn, to explore, and to help others."

Since the X-100 was designed in a top-secret factory in Kinetic City, the vehicle was renamed the **Kinetic City Express** and the first young crew was dubbed the **Kinetic City Super Crew**.

But who would be the members of the Crew? Kinetic City's mayor, Richard M. Schwindle, puts out a call to the young people of the city. Many answer the call, and seven are chosen: Keisha, Derek, Megan, Curtis, Fernando, PJ, and Max.

Now the Crew travel the world, along with their talkative supercomputer ALEC, in a tireless quest for truth, justice, and the perfect deep-dish pizza. Their quest may never end.

About the Train

CIA Top Secret Document #113057
DECLASSIFIED: 9/12/99

Originally designed to carry military intelligence teams to trouble spots throughout the world, the X-100 is capable of ultra-high-speed travel, under the control of the Advanced Logic Electronic Computer (ALEC) Series 9000. The vehicle can travel over land on existing train tracks and on tank-style treads. For crossing bodies of water, the X-100 can seal its waterproof bulkheads and travel underwater, using an advanced form of Magneto-Hydrodynamic Drive propulsion. The X-100 has several small vehicles within it which can travel with or without human passengers, including a small submarine and a jet copter. Finally, the X-100 has sophisticated information-gathering capabilities, using 'round-the-clock, high-speed access to the Internet, an extensive CD-ROM library, and the ability to generate realistic science simulations in its "Cyber Car."

The Phone Call

"Kinetic City Super Crew. When you want the facts, we hit the tracks. Keisha speaking."

"Yah, this is Arnold Rutabegger. I am going to be in a movie!"

"Wow, that's cool, Arnold!"

"No, it is *freezing*! We are making the movie in Alaska. But I am not just shivering because of the cold."

"What do you mean?"

"I am shaking with fear, too! This movie has been cursed!"

CHAPTER ONE

A Chilling Tale

Kinetic City Express Journal: "Snow Problem: The Case of Mushing Madness," Keisha reporting.

Whenever the hotline rings with a call from our old friend Arnold Rutabegger, you can bet the Super Crew is in for a crazy time. Arnold is a very big but not very bright guy. He's a beefy body-builder type--a huge man with huge muscles--but he doesn't have a lot going on upstairs, if you know what I mean. So even though he's so much older and bigger than any of us, Arnold kinda looks up to the Crew. Basically, that means that he's always getting into trouble and asking for our help. This time was no different. He called us from Alaska, of all places, with good news and bad news.

The good news was, Arnold was finally fulfilling his lifelong dream to be in the movies! He had gotten an awesome job, working on a film starring his action movie idol, John-Clod Van Dumm. The bad news was, something was going really wrong with the film's production. Arnold said a bunch of the stunt people had been hurt in various strange accidents. For a big action flick like this one, that meant big trouble.

It also meant that crazy rumors were flying around that the whole production was cursed! That sounded totally silly to me, but poor Arnold was scared stiff. With so many people hurt, the director had given Arnold a chance to do some stunts in the movie. At first, Arnold was totally excited, but now, with his big test stunt just a few days away, he was terrified the curse would get him too.

To make matters worse, poor Arnold was also <u>frozen</u> stiff! His teeth were chattering the whole time we were talking. I tried to calm him down over the phone, but he was just too worked up. He wanted to make a big impression on the director, but he had convinced himself that he was the curse's next victim. It was pretty obvious that the Super Crew was going to have to go up there and look after Arnold in person. Anyway, I couldn't give him the cold shoulder. (Hey, I'll have to tell the Crew that one. Did I tell you I love puns? Maybe even more, I love hearing the rest of the Crew groan at them.)

I knew the other members of the Super Crew would want to help Arnold, too, especially since this case had a glamourous, show biz angle. So I went off to gather them together. Fernando was in the KC Express Train's Video Car, watching a cheesy sci-fi thriller, "Attack of the Deranged Dingoes." Megan was in the Library Car, reading the latest edition of her favorite weekly tabloid magazine, the National Tattler (Their motto: "Stories So Hot You Should Be Reading with an Oven Mitt"). And Curtis, as usual, was tinkering with his latest "improvements" to the train—this time he said he *was getting the heating system in shape, even though it was only early September.*

We all met in the KC Express Train's command headquarters, the Control Car. That's where we always go to discuss new cases with the help of our talking supercomputer ALEC. Fernando came bouncing in first . . .

"Okay, Keisha, what's the spoon?" he said, full of energy.

"The *spoon*?" I replied.

"Yeah, you know, like 'what's the scoop.'"

No, I didn't know, but I was used to being stumped by Fernando's talk. He just loves to use whatever phrase is currently on the trendy-meter. I can usually figure out what he's talking about, but sometimes he just loses me. "Well," I said, "the, uh, spoon is this: we got a call from Arn . . ."

"Oh, wait!" Fernando interrupted. "I forgot to tell you my totally wide new idea! 'Kinetic City Super Crew: The Movie!'"

"What? What are you talking about?" I

asked. Fernando always has some wild idea to liven up the train. Some of them are totally crazy—like the time he wanted to have a weenie roast in the Garden Car. Let's just say that bonfires and automatic sprinkler systems don't mix. Anyway, I figured today's movie epic idea must have been inspired by the cheesy movie he had just been watching.

"Remember the time the Crew helped Claude Cloulez save those whales in Nova Scotia?"

"Sure," I said. "'The Case of the Helpless Humpbacks.' I'll never forget that one. My blue jacket still smells like fish."

"Well I think it would make an awesome adventure movie, and I know just how we can do it! First, I put some toy boats in the bathtub and shoot them in extreme close-up . . ."

I thought Fernando was out of his mind, but while he was talking, Megan walked in. Right away she was hooked. (Get it? Hooked? I kill myself.) "Sounds cool," she began, "but what are we gonna do for whales?"

Fernando was on a roll. "Keisha, doesn't your little sister have a whole bunch of those Bean-Bag Pals? She's gotta have a whale! We can use that."

Megan shook her head furiously. "Wait! Forget the whales," she cried, snapping her fingers. "There's big bucks to be made in disaster flicks. Let's *sink* the boat!"

"Yeah," Fernando agreed. "That's what sells—explosions, disaster, screaming! We'll sink the boat, maybe blow up the train . . ."

Right then, Curtis walked in, totally confused. "Sink the boat? Blow up the train? I don't like the sound of this."

Fernando gave a quick description of his movie—a "high-concept pitch" he called it—but Curtis wasn't interested. "Fernando, man, why don't you use your time more productively? You could give me a hand fixing the train's heating system."

"The heating system? Why are you messing with that, Curtis?" Megan asked suspiciously. "It's not even October yet."

"It's never too early to check things out," he said, a bit defensively. "I'm making sure we don't need any major adjustments before winter comes."

"Yeah," Fernando agreed. "Deep six it. Bail out. Make like a deodorant and roll on."

"It's okay. I can handle it." Curtis responded. "And it's way more important than some lame home movie!"

"Just for that, no free passes to the premiere!" Fernando shot back.

"Boo-hoo," Curtis said sarcastically.

They weren't really mad at each other—it was just teasing—but I stepped in. "Time out, guys! We have a case, remember?"

They both turned and faced me. "Right. What's up with Arnold this time?" Curtis asked.

"Well, here's the deal—he called from Alaska, just outside the town of Fairbanks. His new job is . . ." I hesitated. I didn't want to mention the curse thing just yet. The three of them would have laughed me off the train. "The job is all messed up. And he's really . . . cold." As soon as I said it, I realized how dumb it sounded.

"He called us because he's cold?" Curtis exclaimed.

"And he doesn't like his job?" Fernando added. "And you took me away from my movie for this? Just tell him to quit the job and come home to Kinetic City." He turned toward the exit door.

I tried to stop him. "I know it sounds like an open and shut case, Fernando, but remember, we're talking about Arnold. Sometimes the most obvious answers are beyond him. Besides, in Alaska, staying warm could be a life or death thing."

"Fine," Fernando answered, still heading for the door. "Send him a nice warm coat. I'll be in the Bathroom Car with the video camera. Wait. That didn't come out right . . ."

"Wait, Nando!" I said. I knew he wouldn't want to leave when I told him the rest. "Arnold's in Alaska because he's working on the film crew for a John-Clod Van Dumm movie."

That got him. He was back in the room in a flash. "Did you say 'movie'?"

"Yeah. He's got a chance to be a stunt man, but he's afraid of getting hurt."

"Then what are we waiting for? Let's take those warm clothes to Arnold personally!"

Megan had perked up at the mention of the movie, too. "I'm with Nando," she said. "The sooner we get to that movie set . . . I mean to Arnold, the better."

"I'll fire up ALEC," said Curtis.

By then I knew I couldn't hold back on the curse angle any longer. "Before we go, I should tell you one more thing . . ."

The other three Crew members looked at me suspiciously.

"Well, uh . . ." I knew this was going to get me in trouble. "The main reason Arnold's scared to do his stunt is because he thinks the movie is cursed."

Just as I feared, Fernando started to laugh.

"C'mon, Keisha, we're the Kinetic City Super Crew, not the gang from Scooby-Doo," he chuckled.

"Yeah," Megan said. "Even the *National Tattler* wouldn't run a story that goofy."

Curtis was the only one not laughing. You see, he's a guy who likes all the comforts of civilization. He never met a piece of electronics he didn't like. His idea of roughing it is sleeping without an electric blanket. Not the kind of guy you'd find out in the frozen wilderness. The chance to see a real film shoot had revved him up for a minute, but I think the mention of a curse brought him back to his normal self. "I don't like the sound of that. Why does he think there's a curse?"

"He says there have been some accidents, and people have gotten hurt," I replied. "The production is behind schedule and over budget and everybody's starting to panic."

"There's your problem right there," Fernando commented. "When people panic, they make mistakes."

"Yeah," Megan agreed, "and if they're really cold, too—fumbling with mittens and stuff like that—they probably make even more mistakes."

Fernando smiled. "Let's go up there and straighten things out. Maybe we can get a credit on the film: Curse Consultants."

They were teasing, but at least they were still willing to help. "Okay, let's move," I said, "but before we go, let's make sure we don't have the same problem Arnold has. We'd better find some warm gear. It's freezing there most of the time."

Curtis automatically went into high-tech mode. "I've heard that astronauts have suits that can keep them warm in temperatures 200 degrees below freezing."

Fernando laughed at that one. "That sounds about right. Arnold can be a real space cadet."

"I don't think Arnold needs an astronaut suit," Megan said. "But we probably have some stuff in the Supply Car we can all use. Let's get ALEC going and then we can check it out on the way to Alaska."

I moved to the computer. "Good idea. I'll get ALEC warmed up. Get it—*warmed* up?"

The others looked at me blankly. Not even a groan out of them. "Okay, okay, sorry," I sighed. "Maybe while he gets the train moving, he'll have advice for beating the cold."

ALEC, I should tell you, is the Super Crew's ultra-cool computer. He's got files on every subject under the sun—and probably in other galaxies, too. He's like a giant digital library, with files, databases, graphs, and multimedia abilities that spew out information at a rate that leaves us totally amazed. ALEC's also the computerized auto-pilot of our KC Express Train, which takes us anywhere in the world we need to go for our cases.

I spun around in the swivel seat in front of ALEC and began typing. The rest of the Crew looked up at ALEC's big screen monitor, which fills up one whole wall of the Control Car.

With lights flashing and blinking, ALEC burst to life. "Hellllooooo, Crew. Did you know that dogs have three eyelids?"

The only downside about ALEC, I guess, is that he never just boots up and waits for us to ask him a question. He comes on blazing with some crazy trivia. This time, his screen activated with a huge picture of a dog's head.

"Three eyelids? I'm not sure we need to . . ." I tried to interrupt, but once ALEC gets excited about something, it's hard to stop him. As he spoke, the huge multiscreen monitor flickered with images to illustrate his findings—like mega-close-ups of the dog's eyes. It was kinda gross, actually. But ALEC wasn't about to stop before he shared his latest factoid treasure.

"The main lid and the lower lid function much like yours do, but the third lid—hidden between them in the corner of the dog's eye— can sweep across the eye and clean it, like a windshield wiper."

I tried again to rein him in. "Thanks, ALEC, but we don't have time to talk about dogs right now. We got an urgent call from Arnold Rutabegger in Alaska . . ."

"Ah, Alaska. The Great White North . . ."

Oh, no! This set him off *again*. As ALEC spoke, a stream of multimedia images of Alaska flashed on the screen. "Land of tundras, glaciers, the great gold rush! Home to exotic wildlife like moose, bears, mountain goats, and wolves. Not to mention . . ."

Fernando interrupted. "Don't mention them! We get the point!"

The screens suddenly went blank as ALEC stopped talking. He gave out a wounded sigh as he sputtered to a stop. "Oh. Okay. So what's Arnold's problem this time?"

Megan laid it out. "He's trying to break into the movies, but . . ."

"Breaking into the movies?" WHOOP-WHOOP-WHOOP!! ALEC's Red Alert alarm went off and an obnoxious siren filled the Control Car. "According to Statute 117, Paragraph 3A, any attempt to gain unlawful entry into a theatrical venue is punishable by . . ."

"Stop, ALEC! Stop!" I called out, and the siren, thankfully, wound down to silence. That's another thing about ALEC—he takes everything you say literally. You have to be careful about how you phrase things so he doesn't get confused.

Curtis sighed. "Megan means he's trying to break into the movie *business*, ALEC. And the film he's working on is in Alaska."

"Oh, I see," ALEC said. "I hope he took some warm clothes with him. Alaska can be very cold."

"Actually," I said, "that's one of Arnold's problems, ALEC. He's not dealing with the weather very well."

"I'm not surprised," our computer replied. "Most of Alaska is located in either the Arctic or Subarctic regions. Winters are ferociously cold. From November through March, the temperature often goes to 50 degrees below zero. Summers there are short and cool— only three months of the year average more than 50 degrees Fahrenheit. This being mid-September, there's a good chance he's in subfreezing temperatures." There was a worried 'ping' from ALEC's monitors. "Oh, dear. I hope he doesn't get hypothermia."

"What?" Megan asked.

"Hypothermia," ALEC repeated. "That's the medical term for when you lose body heat faster than it can be replaced. Victims may show warning signs such as confusion, difficulty speaking and shivering."

"Did Arnold sound confused, Keisha?" Curtis asked me.

"No more than usual," I said.

"I don't like the sound of all this." Curtis shivered just hearing about it.

"I don't think it's that bad," I said. "But let's not take any chances. We'd better get there as soon as we can."

Megan had the same idea. "Let's roll, Crew. Arnold wants to be in show business. So let's get up there and help before he gets cold feet."

I couldn't help but laugh. "Cold feet? He's already got them!" This case was going to give everyone pun fever—whether they wanted it or not!

After a good round of groans at my razor-sharp wit, Megan leaned over my shoulder to tap a few keys to get ALEC rolling. "Pardon me, Pun Princess," she said. "ALEC, set course, please. North, to Fairbanks, Alaska!"

"You bet, Megan!" ALEC chirped happily. His sensitive circuits responded at once, boosting the train's engines into action. And with that, the KC Express revved up and hurtled us toward the Great White North. Curse or no curse, we were on our way.

CHAPTER TWO

Bundle Up!

Even at the high speeds of the Kinetic City
Express Train, we knew that it would take
some time to get all the way to Alaska, so we
headed for the Supply Car to suit up in some
cold weather gear.

The KC Express has an awful lot of cars,
so many I've never even counted them.
Unfortunately, the Supply Car was pretty far
back, since it was full of stuff that we didn't
use very often. In fact, we sometimes joked
that we should call it the Attic Car, 'cause it
was kinda dusty and out of the way.

As we walked through one car to another,
making our way from the Control Car back to the
Supply Car, I noticed a chill in the air . . .

"Has anyone noticed that it's getting colder?" I wondered out loud as we left the Gym Car.

"Of course it is," Curtis replied matter-of-factly. "We're going north. The climate gets colder."

"But we're in the KC Express Train!" I said. "After all, we *do* have a heating system . . ." And then I suddenly remembered Curtis's efforts to "check out" the system. ". . . or at least, we *did* until someone started messing around with it."

Fernando, Megan, and I all turned at once to see if Curtis had anything to say. By the look on his face, we knew he was guilty.

"Okay, so I disconnected the heating system. But it was only supposed to be temporary while I worked on the thermostat . . ."

Megan arched an eyebrow. "And then what happened, Inventor-Boy?"

Curtis looked down, "Well, I thought I knew where every piece came from, so I could put it all back together again, but when

I was finished . . ." He rubbed the toe of his sneaker against the floor, ". . . there were a couple of extra pieces." He looked up quickly. "But I'm sure I can fix it. I just need some time!"

"C'mon, Einstein," Megan said with a groan. "Now we really need to get some warm clothes."

We hurried on, but Curtis bailed as we passed through the Lab Car. "You guys go on. I want to pack some stuff for the trip," he announced. By "stuff" I knew he meant he was going to fill up his backpack with the usual assortment of strange gadgets he was always inventing. Too bad most of them are a waste of space.

"No more messing with the heating system!" Megan warned. "I'm really getting cold now."

Fernando was shivering, too. "Yeah, and get down to the Supply Car as soon as you can. You're gonna need a coat until we get the heat back on."

We kept walking, through the Library Car, the Garage Car, the Lounge Car, the Observatory Car, and so on. And on. And on. Until at last we came to the Supply Car. Fernando climbed up on a step-ladder to reach a high shelf of cartons marked "Winter Gear" and tossed down two of the boxes. I sorted through the first one, pulling out gloves and scarves and thick, rubber-soled boots to find sets for each of us in the right sizes. Megan, meanwhile, went into the back to find the parkas and snow pants.

Curtis rejoined us just as we were finished sorting through the boots. He was carrying a heavy backpack that rattled and clanked. "Anybody want to see what I've got in here?" he asked hopefully.

"Okay," I teased. "What's in your bag of tricks this time?"

He smiled like a magician reaching for the rabbit in his top hat. The backpack was stuffed with his usual assortment of unusual items. The first thing he pulled out looked a lot like some kind of super-jumbo water gun.

"What the heck is that?" I asked, nervously. Since Curtis's inventions usually backfire, anything that looked like a weapon made the rest of the Crew very uneasy.

"I call it the 'Winter Wilderness Automatic Trail Tagger,'" Curtis replied.

"Oh," Fernando said, still wary. "What does it *do*?"

Curtis was ready. "Well, you know how people sometimes get lost in the woods if they're not on a clearly marked trail?"

We all nodded.

"Well, as you're walking, this baby lays down a thin trail of colored gravel—I filled it with the stuff that goes in the bottom of fish-tanks—so that you can easily retrace your steps back home. Isn't that great?"

"It sounds like Hansel and Gretel to me," Fernando laughed.

"C'mon, guys, gimme a break," Curtis said. "I'm not using breadcrumbs, here. This is a real tool that could save somebody's life. Remember what ALEC said about hypothermia?"

"*Somebody's* life?" I teased. "Or yours? You've never been real keen for hiking into any dark forests . . . or Alaskan tundras."

"C'mon, Keisha, lighten up." Curtis turned to Megan. "There's a big business in hiking and camping gear," he told her.

Megan's eyes lit up with interest. "Hmmmm . . . You *might* be able to market a gadget like that. Let me see it." She took the device from Curtis and hefted it in her hands. "Lightweight, but sturdy. Not bad, Curtis."

"Be careful there, Megan," Curtis warned. "There's no safety latch on the . . ."

Too late! A spray of gravel shot across the Supply Car, hitting the train's metal walls with a loud, skittering sound. Luckily, I was standing behind Megan, and Fernando ducked just in time to avoid getting hit by the cloud of tiny rocks.

We all turned to glare at Curtis. He smiled. "Okay, so I have to adjust the intensity of the gravel dispensing system. At least we know it works, right?"

I was ready to tell Curtis that I was tired of his goofy inventions—especially the ones that could draw blood!—but I knew it wasn't going to change his mind. "Whatever," I said. "Just don't ask me to carry any of that junk."

I'm sure he would have jumped to defend his latest creations, but the train's PA system clicked on to announce our destination. "Now arriving—Fairbanks, Alaska. Don't forget your snowshoes!"

"All right! Let's get moving!" Fernando said, rubbing his hands together excitedly. "Watch out, Hollywood, I'm ready for my close-up."

And with that, we left the train and walked into the brilliant white, frozen landscape.

CHAPTER THREE

The Fall Guy

We arrived in Fairbanks, Alaska, in the middle of the day. But even though the sun was shining brightly, the temperature was below freezing and a brisk wind made it feel even colder. It was hard to believe it was only September--it felt like the middle of winter to me.

We looked around, getting our bearings. Fairbanks is the second largest city in Alaska, located in the heart of the Interior Plateau-- that's the large, rolling uplands in the middle of the state. It's a busy city, a transportation center for all the surrounding regions, including the Arctic, because it's got the Alaska Railroad, four highways, and the Chena River all within a small distance.

This part of Alaska doesn't have many trees, but there were large open spaces of what's called "tundra"--land covered with mosses, grasses, small flowering plants, and shrubs. In the distance, we could see the great Alaska Range, a mountain barrier dominated by Mount McKinley--the tallest mountain in North America.

It was gorgeous territory, all right, and I was psyched to be there--but Curtis didn't share my excitement . . .

"Brrrrr," Curtis stomped his boots in the snow. "This is *not* my kind of weather. Let's find Arnold and get back inside ASAP!"

Megan pointed to a spot in the near distance, just outside of town. "My bet is, he's over there."

We looked that way and saw a beehive of activity—lots of lights and trucks and crowds of people milling around. The arrival of John-Clod Van Dumm and his film crew was obviously the biggest thing to happen to Fairbanks in ages.

"So if Arnold is just now getting his chance to do some stunts, what was he hired to do in the first place?" Megan asked.

I filled them in on the little I knew. "You know, I'm not sure," I answered. "He only told me about working with John-Clod Van Dumm's personal stunt double. Some guy with a real tough-sounding name—Brick or Rock or something . . ."

Fernando's eyes grew wide. "Was it Brock?"

I nodded. "Yeah, that sounds about right."

"Brock Hardley?" he said, barely holding back a shout.

"Yeah, that's it." I said. "That's the guy Arnold's working with."

"This gets more wicked all the time! The man's a living legend!" Fernando was really pumped. "Brock Hardley's been in some of my absolute favorite films! He was the head zombie in 'Death Rides the Roller Coaster!' And then he was the demonic plumber in 'Don't Go Near the Sewer!' Man, I love this case!"

"Don't get star-struck, Fernando," I warned him. "We have a job to do, remember?"

"Don't spill your milk, Keisha. I'm tight on close-up!"

"What?" I asked.

"That's filmmaking lingo for 'I'm on it!'"

We gently pushed through a ring of onlookers who were checking out that day's on-location shoot. Inside that circle, there was another group of people, wearing headsets and carrying clipboards. They looked and acted important, but they didn't seem to be doing much at all. And dead center, we saw Van Dumm and some other actors. As we worked our way to the heart of the action, Megan pointed to a guy wearing a familiar gray "KC Gym" sweatsuit. "There's Arnold right there!"

He noticed us, too, and came running toward us. As soon as we got a good, close look at him, it was pretty obvious why he was so cold. That "KC Gym" sweatsuit was the *only* thing he was wearing. As he hustled toward us, he was wringing his hands, thumping his chest, and jumping up and down, trying to stay warm.

"Oh, Super Crew, I am so happy to see you!" he said with a sniffle. But he didn't look very happy. In fact, he looked miserable. He was shaking like a leaf and the dark circles around his eyes told me he hadn't been sleeping well lately. "Ever since I have come here, I have been so cold and trembly. Quick! Come with me back near the big lights, so I can warm up."

"Uh, Arnold," Megan said, "not to point out the obvious or anything, but we're in *Alaska*! Why aren't you wearing a coat?"

"I will explain everything, Crew. But please, let's go under the toasty lights!"

He began walking toward a large bank of overhead lights to the left of all the activity and we stepped in line with him. But I'll admit, it was hard to concentrate on conversation. There was all this strange equipment—huge lighting rigs, camera cranes, boom mics, and all sorts of high-tech pieces of gray steel and black metal. The machines, the noise, the frenzied bustling of people in costume—it was all so exciting, and distracting.

"Wow, a real movie set!" Fernando exclaimed. "Arnold, how did you get this phenominous break?"

Arnold's already massive chest puffed up with pride. "I am lucky, yes. I work directly with the director of this major motion picture."

Megan, whose always had a nose for big-time business, show or otherwise, was clearly impressed. "Really? You're right there as those important—and expensive—movie-making decisions are made?"

Arnold beamed. "Yah. The director needs me nearby or he cannot work. I am unvaluable."

Curtis and I exchanged a glance. Despite being in America for over ten years now, Arnold still has trouble with the language sometimes. "Don't you mean *in*valuable?" Curtis asked gently.

Arnold nodded. "Yah. I am that, too. Especially with the curse and all."

"Oh, boy, here we go with the curse thing," Fernando said. "Okay, Arnold, spill it."

"But I am not holding anything," Arnold said, bewildered.

"He means tell us what's up with this so-called curse," Megan explained. "Where did you get such a loopy idea?"

"Oh, I see," Arnold began. "One of the reasons I have this most fantastical chance to do a stunt was because of all the accidents. Except only for Brock, every stunt person has had something bad happen."

"Are they okay?" Curtis gulped. "Did anyone die?"

"No, thanks to the heavens," Arnold replied. "But many broken bones and bad boo-boos. So many things have gone wrong on this movie, the crew says it must be cursed."

"Arnold, you realize this whole curse thing is crazy, don't you?" I demanded.

He looked down, nervously. "But . . ."

Suddenly, there was a commotion, and we heard shouts from the set. A heavy-set man in flashy sunglasses and a thick, salt-and-pepper colored beard was waving his arms impatiently as assistants scattered in all directions.

"Okay, okay, places everyone. And I want absolute quiet while Brock gets ready for his stunt!"

"Ah, that is the director, Cameron Martin Hoppola . . ." Arnold began.

"Of course he is! I'd know that beard anywhere!" Fernando gushed. "He's the man who made 'The Goonfather' and 'Days of Ignorance' and 'Down with the Big Canoe.' The guy's a genius!"

Arnold nodded, pleased at Fernando's enthusiasm. "Yah. Und the other man, the tall blond one . . ."

"That's Brock Hardley, right?" Fernando said.

"Yah," Arnold confirmed. "Mr. Van Dumm's personal stunt double und my new personal boss. He is a movie legend, too. He has broken every bone in his body at least once in doing his incredible stunts."

Brock was an older guy, probably in his fifties, with a handsome but tough face and bleached blond hair. He was joking with a reporter and a photographer. From the logo stitched on the back of their leather jackets, I could see they were from *Movie Times* magazine.

Brock walked away from the journalists and then yelled back, loud enough for all the bystanders to hear. "I'm going four stories up on that man-made mountain and I'm riding up *slow*. But I'm coming back down in one swift sweep, so you'd better have some high-speed film in that camera!"

The crowd laughed. The reporter and photographer hastily took their positions to watch the stunt. The rest of us did too.

When we first got to the set, there had been a lot of noise—people chattering and machines clanking—but as Brock made his way to the top of the snowy hill, a hush fell over the crowd. Suddenly, the clipboard people scurried into position, like it was some kind of military exercise, and a few people on walkie-talkies whispered in tense, hushed tones. It was like at the circus when the trapeze artist goes high over the audience and everyone holds their breath.

"What's he gonna do, Arnold?" I asked.

"He is going to ski down the mountain and take off from that ramp there . . ." Arnold pointed to a wooden ramp that jutted out about half-way down the side of the snow-covered hill. I imagined Brock flying off that ramp and jumping out into the sky, but I didn't see any place for him to land.

"But where does he come down?" Curtis wondered.

"Quiet on the set!" Hoppola yelled, and Curtis clammed up tight.

"You will see," Arnold whispered.

Now we were totally confused. A man stepped forward, in front of the camera. He was holding one of those movie clacker things that announces the beginning of a shot. "Copter Catch, Take One," he said. Then a loud buzzer sounded. This was it! Everyone's eyes went up to the top of the ski jump.

Brock had strapped on a pair of racing skis and was waiting for the director's signal. Hoppola put his hand up and, after a dramatic pause, dropped it, like the guy who waves the checkered flag at the start of a car race.

At that, Brock pushed off, and came tearing down the hill. At just the same time, I heard a roaring sound and saw a helicopter climbing into the sky from behind the hill, a cameraman leaning out the side.

As Brock came hurtling toward the ski jump, I still had no idea where he could possibly land. Then I realized that he was heading straight toward us! Why was everyone standing around? Why didn't they get out of the way?

Curtis and I exchanged a worried glance, but Megan and Fernando stood, frozen in place (hey, another cold pun!), watching as Brock flew off the edge of the ski jump and into the sky.

"Man, that helicopter's getting awfully close to Brock . . ." I began, and then the truth hit me—Brock wasn't going to land, at least not here. He was actually aiming *for* the helicopter!

Maybe all the people in the film crew knew what was going to happen, but they gasped anyway. Brock twisted in the air and positioned himself to come in just under the helicopter, near the bottom runners. With amazing, split-second timing, he grabbed the runners and stopped in mid-flight. For a few moments, as the copter circled the crowd and moved on, he dangled there as the cameraman leaned out of the doorway and shot more film.

Brock hung onto the helicopter runners, swinging from side to side, as if looking around nervously. Then, suddenly, he clutched his hand to his chest, like he'd been shot. With an anguished cry, he went limp and just . . . dropped! Straight down, at least 60 or 70 feet!

I couldn't help it—I screamed.

Fernando poked me in the side, and pointed to the ground below the copter. "Check it out. The man's not crazy."

A big camera crane had blocked it before, but now I could see a huge, six-foot high air-bag, positioned just under the spot where the helicopter hovered. All around the edges of the pillow was padding, like the exercise mats you'd use at the gym.

The fall took only a few seconds, but it seemed like forever as we watched the man fall out of the sky. He went straight down, like a rock, and then disappeared into the huge air bag.

"Hey, it's like jumping onto a huge bed!" Curtis laughed out loud. I thought there'd be a cheer, but still the crowd was quiet. No one moved. Even the crew members held their breath. What was wrong?

"Is he okay, Arnold?" I asked nervously.

Arnold just stared at the air bag. The huge pillow had stopped shaking, but there was still no sign of Brock. "He should have moved by now," Arnold said, his voice getting high and squeaky. "Oh, no! He must be hurt, or even . . ." He took a gasp of breath. "Maybe the curse has cursed Brock, too!"

CHAPTER FOUR

Hey, Arnold!

Those few moments, standing on the movie set, waiting for some signal that Brock was all right, seemed to go on forever. But just when we were convinced that there had been some kind of terrible accident, I saw a hand waving in the air from the middle of the air bag. Then Brock peered out at the crowd and smiled. "Scared ya, didn't I?" he said with a mischievous grin.

The crowd broke out in relieved cheers. The crew started to applaud, and one guy put down his clipboard long enough to offer Brock a hand. Brock slapped it a high five. Then he pulled on the guy's hand to get his balance while he removed the skis, and jumped off the air bag, back to the ground.

Fernando was cheering loudest of all. He ran forward to personally congratulate his hero. The rest of us stood, talking about the stunt with Arnold . . .

"That was incredible," Curtis said, still stunned by the stunt. "Even with that airbag, you couldn't pay me enough money to risk my life like that."

"Yah, Brock is fearless," Arnold said. "Und he says he will teach me to be fearless, so I can do a stunt in the movie, too."

Just then, a loud, angry voice broke through the film set chatter.

"Where's my hot chocolate? Where's the hot chocolate boy?" It was Cameron Martin Hoppola and he was mad!

Arnold snapped to attention. "Ooops. I must go." He turned anxiously, and started toward the bearded man.

Megan grabbed Arnold's arm, holding him back briefly. "You're the hot chocolate boy?" She teased. "That's the job that brought you all the way to Alaska?"

Arnold tried to put his best spin on this revelation. "Yah, but now I am a slasher!"

We all looked at him, shocked, waiting for an explanation.

"I think that is the word . . .," Arnold began, "for a person who does more than one thing only. Like a writer-slash-director. I am a hot chocolate boy-slash-stunt man. Except I am not yet a stunt man. Yet. We will talk more later."

Then he turned and started jogging toward the director, stopping quickly at a cafe cart near the side of the set. But before he got out of earshot he turned back to face us. In a deadpan voice, he announced, "I'll be back."

"It's kinda pitiful, isn't it?" Curtis chuckled.

Megan shrugged. "I dunno. I heard Julia Roberts got her big break catching bullfrogs for a remake of 'Huckleberry Finn' . . ."

"After every shot is in the can, I want hot chocolate, and I want it immediately!" the director yelled, in a voice loud enough to be heard back in Kinetic City.

"I don't think anybody ever yelled at Julia Roberts like that," I said, as we hurried closer to see what was wrong. Poor Arnold. He just stood silently, hanging his head while the director bellowed at him.

"Ruttabeenie! Ruttabeenie! Ruttabeenie! How many times do I have to tell you—hold the marshmallows!"

Arnold shuffled nervously in place. "That's Rutabegger, Rutabegger, Rutabegger, Mr. Hoppola, Hoppola, Hoppola. Director. Sir."

"Oh, whatever!" The smaller, much tougher man turned away in a huff. "I knew I shouldn't have let Brock give you a stunt assignment while you were on beverage detail. That's like asking you to walk and chew gum at the same time."

Arnold nodded eagerly. "But I can do that." He paused. "As long as I don't have to blow bubbles, too."

Mr. Hoppola just sighed. "So what about the stunt, Rotobeenie? Brock said you were going to show me what you could do. When do I see it?"

"Soon. Soon. Any day now, Sir." Arnold was obviously stalling. "We are planning something *wunderbar!*"

Mr. Hoppola was unconvinced. "Yeah, yeah. Like what?"

"Something for the big chase scene. I will run from the bad guys, jump onto a dog sled, and race through the town!"

Mr. Hoppola nodded impatiently. "Yeah? And then what?"

Arnold looked frantic. It was pretty obvious he hadn't planned anything beyond the dog sled chase. "And then . . . uh . . . the dogs and I will race over that tiny, rickety bridge over there . . ."

The director nodded, waiting for more. "What about some firepower, eh? A little apoc-alyptic POW?!"

". . . uh, und then I will activate a grenade with my teeth and chuck it into the river. Okay?"

The director mulled it over. "Chase. Sled. Race. Grenade. Explosion." He paused, running his fingers thoughtfully through his thick bead. Then, in a booming voice, "I *like* it!"

Arnold's nodding mechanism was in overdrive. "You *will* like it! Yah! You will give it two thumbs up! Way, way up!" he exclaimed.

Hoppola put up his hand. "Down boy, down." He waited until Arnold was standing perfectly still and hanging on his next words. "You got *three* days."

Arnold went back to nodding furiously. "Yessirr! I will practice!" He was jumping up and down, ready to take off.

"And one more thing, Ratatooie," Hoppola added sternly. "Use a *fake* grenade. We'll add the explosion in post-production."

Arnold seemed disappointed. "Really? No KA-BOOM?"

"This film is behind schedule and over budget as it is," the director grumbled. "Can't have you risking your fool neck. You're the only stunt man I've got left, after Brock. Now get moving!"

"Okay, Mr. Hoppola, director, sir." As Arnold headed off, Hoppola glanced at the huge crowd of crew people that was watching his every move. "People, people, people!" he yelled. He was clearly a guy who liked to order folks around. "What's everyone standing around for? We've got a movie to make!" He lifted a megaphone to his lips (not that he needed one) and shouted, "Everyone in place for the end of the world sequence! Take 47!"

As he walked away through a throng of extras, they scattered like he was cutting a path right through them. It reminded me of a movie I saw where Moses parted the Red Sea and walked through without getting a drop on him.

Arnold rushed over to tell us his news. "Did you hear that, Super Crew? I will be crawling up the ladder of stardom soon. Brrrr . . . if I don't freeze first! Right now I can barely wriggle my fingers to open the box of hot chocolate mix!"

Megan patted his arm gently. "Don't worry, Arnold. You'll be okay. We're here to help."

"Oh, I hope so," the big man blubbered. "I have been so cold up here, I can hardly do my workouts. And if my muscles get flabby . . ." he paused, and let out a little sob, as if such a thing were too horrible to contemplate. ". . . then I will become not muscly."

Fernando walked up while Arnold whimpered. He had Brock Hardley with him. You could see that the older guy and his young fan were already hitting it off, big time. Fernando was practically jumping out of his boots as he introduced us all to the stunt man. "Crew, it is my insane privilege to introduce you to Mr. Brock 'the Rock' Hardley."

You could see how much the stunt man enjoyed Fernando's enthusiasm. He was beaming as he shook Curtis's hand, and he even kind of bowed to Megan and me, kissing our hands like some old-time country gentlemen. Megan was starstruck and beamed right back at him. I guess I'm just not the hooray-for-Hollywood type. I thought it was all a little much.

"So, did you enjoy the martini?" Brock asked us.

"Uh, Mr. Hardley, sir. The Super Crew is too young to drink," Arnold nervously mentioned.

"I know that, Arnold," Brock laughed loudly. "That's a show-business term. The martini is the last shot of the day."

"Cool. More film lingo!" Fernando cried. You could see him making a mental note of that one.

"Of course, after that kind of martini," Brock went on, "I look forward to a hot chocolate back at my trailer. So if you'll excuse me . . ." He bowed his head slightly and walked off, but stopped to say one last thing to Fernando. "If you want that autographed script, son, just stop by tomorrow. It'd be my pleasure."

I've never seen Fernando so happy. "The dude is awesome!" he gushed after Brock left. "You think a guy that tough would be a total snobbus and hard to talk to, but he's totally mellow."

"He seemed nice enough," I said.

"Are you kidding? He's my new major! He was totally thumped when I asked him all about the movies he starred in."

"Thumped?" Curtis asked. "Is that good?"

"Oh yeah!" Fernando exclaimed. "He was blown away!"

"That reminds me, Fernando," Megan interrupted. "Why would a guy go from being a star to a stunt man? Doesn't it usually work the other way around?"

"Yeah," Fernando replied. "But Brock's big roles weren't what you'd call A-list movies. More like straight-to-video stuff. And I think as he got older, those jobs got harder to find."

"Yah, that is true," Arnold agreed. "Brock told me he needed to find different work after his last movie, 'Dawn of the Spawn,' made him a box-office laughing stocking."

"You mean laughing *stock*," Curtis corrected.

"Okay. That, too," Arnold said. "Now Brock says he will work with other stunt peoples to make sure they can follow in his footsteps."

Fernando smiled. "Yeah, he even has some

kind of charity that helps take care of stunt people who get hurt on the job."

Arnold bowed his head respectfully. "Yes, Brock is a wonderful man. When all the other stunt men got hurt and had to go back home, he said I might have what it takes to do the job."

"You mean your muscles and gym training?" I asked.

"No. He said I had the brains to be a stunt man. Isn't that nice?"

We just smiled. I suppose it could be considered a compliment of sorts. "Speaking of brains, Arnold," Fernando said, "where were yours when you picked out these clothes? I mean, a sweatsuit in this weather?"

"You do not like my gray sweatsuit? But it brings out my eyes."

"It's not that, Arnold," I said. "It's that you need to be dressed a lot warmer. I don't think you needed us to come all the way up here just to tell you that."

"But, I am building up my toughness," Arnold replied. "I must learn to feel no pain.

And it must be working, because I can't feel any of my fingers or my nose."

"That's ridiculous, Arnold," Curtis said. "Getting frostbite is no way to train to do stunts."

"Brock told me that pain is the price you pay to be a stunt man." Arnold hesitated, and then grinned hopefully. "Maybe I can pay a discount price, with not so much pain."

Fernando patted Arnold on the back. "I doubt Brock was talking about actual, physical pain, Arnold. I know all about movies—especially action-packed, blow 'em ups. There're plenty of ways stunt people keep from getting hurt. They make it look hard but they play it safe. And I'm pretty sure they all wear coats when it's cold."

Arnold stared at Fernando with new respect. "Do you really think so, Fernando?" He looked at the rest of us. "Crew?"

We all nodded back, encouragingly. "Yes, and if you really want to go through with this, we're here to help," Megan said.

Arnold stomped his foot and clapped his hands decisively. "I want to be in the movies! I will make you proud, Super Crew!" He hesitated. "Do you perhaps know anything about mushing?"

"Mushing? Is that a cooking term?" Curtis shook his head, like he wasn't sure he'd heard it right. "Like mushed potatoes?"

He hadn't.

"No, I mean like doggies pulling sleds," Arnold answered.

"I got it, Arnold," Fernando jumped in. "Musher is the word for people who ride dog sleds on snow."

"I thought dog sleds went out with covered wagons," Megan said. "Does anybody still use those things?"

"Yah," Arnold nodded. "Many of the Alaskan people I have met use dog sleds for transportation. As they say, when in Nome, do as the Nomans do!"

"Um, Arnold, this is Fairbanks," Megan reminded him.

"Oh, yah. Then do as the Fairbankians do!"

"Why would anybody still use a dog sled?" Curtis asked. "Don't they have cars? Or at least snowmobiles?"

"Curtis, those things can be useless in heavy-duty snow," Fernando replied patiently. "Dog sleds can be the only way to get through it."

"How do you know so much, Nando?" I wondered.

Fernando explained. "I saw a show about the Iditarod one night when I was channel surfing. Amazing stuff."

"The Idita-what?" Megan asked.

"The Iditarod!" Fernando exclaimed. "It's a huge dog race—over a thousand miles long. It takes days!"

"Nando is right," Arnold replied. "The race is a fiercely fierce test of mushing skill."

"And now you're going to be a mush-master yourself," Fernando said. "That is so wide!"

"'Mush-Master Arnold.' Yah, I like the sound of that."

"First things first, Arnold," Curtis warned. "If you're going to master this stunt job, you'd better practice."

"Yah." Arnold nodded earnestly. "I must try again to train my mush puppies."

"You already have a dog team?" I asked, surprised.

"Oh, yah," Arnold nodded happily. "The film crew gave me a team of sledding dogs to work with. They are my darling doggies!"

"Well, what are we waiting for?" Fernando asked. "Let's check 'em out. Haw Haw!"

Arnold looked concerned. "Do you need a hankie, Fernando?"

Fernando shook his head and laughed. "No, it's a mushing term. It means 'move on out!'"

Arnold broke out into a huge grin. "Okey pokey!" he announced happily. "Come and meet my mush puppies!"

CHAPTER FIVE

Mush Puppies

It was exciting just to be in Alaska while a major motion picture was being filmed, but to make it even better, our friend Arnold Ruttebegger was preparing to be in it! All he had to do was perform a stunt. Well, actually it wasn't that simple--he had to know how to handle a real Alaska dog sled, among other tricks. We followed him to his temporary Alaskan home to meet his mushing dogs.

    As we walked, he told us his exciting adventures on the movie set. This job was the chance of a lifetime, he admitted, but thanks to the "curse," he was afraid that his lifetime was going to be cut short. We tried to explain *to Arnold that his imagination was running away with him . . .*

"Arnold, you may be working on an action-thriller, but life isn't really like that," I tried to reason with him.

"Take if from me, Arnold," Megan added, "there hasn't been a single mention of the curse in the *National Tattler*, and they cover all the hottest Hollywood news."

I wasn't sure whether I wanted Megan using the *Tattler* to prove anything, but at least Arnold was calming down.

"I will try not to be so superstitious," he said meekly. "But I am trying so hard to get my foot in the door of show business." Arnold looked down and stared glumly at his shoes. "And my little toes are so cold, I can barely move . . ."

We all took a look at Arnold's feet. The whole sweatsuit thing had distracted us so much, we hadn't even looked at his feet before now. He was wearing high-top basket-ball shoes!

"Arnold!" I exclaimed. "Why are you wearing basketball shoes in this snow?"

Arnold was offended. "These are not ordinary sneakers!" he said grandly. "These are Mickey Simpson Air Pump Kabongs. They help me run faster and jump higher!"

"But do they keep your feet warm?" Curtis put it to him simply.

Now Arnold seemed embarrassed. "No, not at all." Then he brightened. "But they're totally stylin'!"

"That's not the point, Arnold," Fernando replied. "You have to dress for the climate you're in. And I don't see any basketball courts around here."

"Yeah, get some boots, big guy," Megan added.

"Okey Pokey," Arnold said. Then, he stopped short. "And here we are. My happy but very chilly home." He opened the door to a sweet little stone cabin.

Funny, but I had the strangest feeling I had seen it before. Of course, that wasn't possible.

I'd never even been to Alaska until this case happened. But I couldn't shake a weird feeling that I knew the place somehow.

It was majorly cold inside, barely warmer than the cold air outside. There wasn't much to see—a cot in the corner, a tiny kitchen area, a poster of John-Clod Van Dumm taped to the wall. And dogs. About a dozen barking, running, yelping dogs. They rushed forward to greet Arnold, bounding up to lick his face. And then they turned to us newcomers, jumping up to sniff our hands and begging to be patted.

Curtis was the first to notice something strange about the sled team. "Arnold, are these really your sled dogs?"

Arnold played with the dogs as he talked about them. "Yah, sure. Pinky and Binky here are Great Danes, and Edna and Vincent and Milly are greyhounds. Those are very fast runners, you know. And the rest are dalmations."

"Like in that movie, 'Dozens of Dotted Doggies,'" Megan said.

Arnold nodded proudly. "Yah, some of these doggies already have film experience."

I looked again at the collection of canines. Sure, they seemed like happy, healthy dogs. But none of them struck me as the kind you'd need for mushing. "And they can really pull you on a sled?" I asked Arnold.

He sighed. "Not yet. Und I blame myself. I am too big and beefy, I think. I have tried to pump them up, but they just want to play. And when I put them in their heavy sweaters so they do not get chilled in the snow, they do not move so good."

I stopped to picture Arnold on the runners of a sled being led by these dogs, bundled up in heavy sweaters. When I looked around, I saw the other Crew members shaking their heads mournfully. They had the same mental image.

Megan voiced it for all of us. "Arnold, sled dogs don't wear sweaters."

Arnold looked at his dogs, confused. "Then how do they keep warm?"

Fernando smiled. "Fur keeps them warm."

"Fernando!" Arnold was shocked. "I do not believe in buying furs!"

I stepped in. "No, Arnold. Fernando means that you should use dogs that have lots of thick, natural fur. All of these dogs have short, wiry coats. They're not bred for this kind of weather, or work."

His face went blank. Then a small line of recognition crossed his brow. "You mean shaggy doggies?"

Fernando nodded. "And strong, tough ones that have been trained for the job. On that TV show I saw about the Iditarod race, the dogs looked like wolves, or huskies. These dogs don't look like sled dogs at all."

"Yeah," Megan said, "I think maybe your movie pals picked good-looking dogs instead of the ones that were right for the job. Typical, huh? Even dogs have to be beautiful in the movies."

The rest of the Crew chuckled a bit at that, but Arnold looked worried and confused. "Oh dear, what do I do now? When I got the stunt job, these are the doggies they gave me."

As Arnold spoke, one of the larger dogs, the Great Dane he called Binky, ran across the room and jumped up against Fernando. He was taken by surprise and fell back, toward the wall. Fernando put his hand out to break his fall— and it went right through the stone!

We all rushed forward to help, but luckily, Fernando wasn't hurt. "Wow," he said, shaking his head in disbelief and staring at his hand. "I don't know my own strength. Punching through a stone wall?!"

Curtis was the first to notice the small dark flakes that had fallen from the hole. "Look at this!" he cried in amazement. "This isn't rock dust or anything hard like that." He squished a few of the tiny pieces in his fingers. "This is . . . cardboard!"

"You're right." Fernando rapped his knuckles against the wall. "And so is this . . ."

Megan walked to another wall and struck it gently. "And this, too."

Sure enough, after we examined the entire cabin, we realized that it was constructed out of cardboard blocks painted to look like rock. It wasn't a real home at all—it was a movie set!

"That's why I know this place," I cried out. "It's the Enrights' house. The one from that TV show, 'Little Cabin in the Canyon'!"

Curtis had wandered into the kitchen area, and tapped his knuckles on the top of the oven. "Even the stove is made from cardboard."

Arnold slapped his hand to his forehead. "That's why my TV dinners never cooked right."

Curtis turned to Arnold. "Why are you living *here*?"

"Is this where the film people set you up?" Megan was angry. "I can't believe it!"

Arnold was surprised at our reactions. "I am sure it was just a mistake. The film people offered me a room in the hotel with the rest of the film crew, but Brock thought that it would be good to stay close to my mush puppies. And when I saw this place, they seemed to like it."

"But Arnold . . ." Curtis was trying to find a way to explain the facts of cold, Alaskan life to the simple strongman. "You're basically living in a cardboard box! No wonder it's so cold in here."

Arnold took a moment to absorb the information. "I should move," he announced with a determined nod of his head. But then, the thought passed (as many, unfortunately, do with Arnold) and a new one put a worried wrinkle on his face. "And you were saying my doggies are being bad?'"

"No, Arnold. They're very nice dogs," I reassured him. "But I don't think they're right for your stunt job."

"I'll say," Fernando added. "I think Arnold's definitely barking up the wrong tree with this dog team."

"So, what do we do now?" Megan asked, patting one of the dalmations on the head.

We all stood in silent thought. Well, Arnold just stood.

Then I had an inspiration. "Remember that dog race Nando was talking about?" I asked, excitedly. "Where did it take place?"

"Here in Alaska," Fernando answered.

"Just what I thought. Maybe we could find a local racer who could help Arnold with a dog sled."

"Great idea, Keisha!" Curtis said.

"Let's head back to the train," Megan said. "We can ask ALEC to check his database for someone in the area. What do you think, Arnold?"

Arnold could sense that we were talking about getting help—and possibly moving to a new, warmer location, so he was all for it. "Oh yes! Do do that Crew thing that you do so well. I must prove myself a hunky chunky stunt man—or stay a hot chocolate boy forever!"

CHAPTER SIX

Chillin' with ALEC

We hurried back to the KC Express Train to
check with ALEC about finding a dog sled
racer in the area. But when we got back to
the train, we could barely open the door
to the Control Room. It was almost frozen
shut!

We had to scrape away a thin layer of
ice, using the sharp plastic edge of Megan's
library card, and even then it took a few
minutes of frantic pulling to get the door
open.

We raced into the Control Car, which felt
like an icebox, and booted ALEC up. It took
an extra few seconds for him to come on. For
a moment, we were really afraid that the

*cold might have ruined his circuits. We all
sighed with relief when we heard that familiar
voice . . .*

"Brrrrrr . . . . . . helllllloooooo, Crew," ALEC
said, his voice a little deeper than usual. "Is it
chilly in here, or is it just me?"

"No, it's not just you," Megan said, glaring
at Curtis. "Somebody must have broken the
heating system."

"Ohhh," ALEC said with a nervous "PING."
"Why would anyone want to break our heating
system?"

"I didn't mean to do it!" Curtis cried out. "It
was an accident, okay? I was doing the standard
fall maintenance check."

ALEC's circuits purred contentedly. "Ah . . .
Good thinking, Curtis."

"Good thought, bogus action," Fernando
commented with a slight shiver. "Remember
the old saying, 'if it ain't broke, don't fix it!'"

ALEC's monitor came to life with a barrage
of pictures of laboratories and construction

sites. "But, Fernando, where would we be without exploration and experimentation?"

"We'd be warm," Nando noted wryly.

"But Curtis is following in the footsteps of some great minds," ALEC replied. With a proud smile on his face, Curtis patted ALEC's keyboard as if to say thanks.

"Yes," ALEC went on, "it reminds me of stories I heard about Dr. Alexander Graham Cracker, the brilliant scientist who created me . . ."

"You tell 'em, ALEC," Curtis said.

"Yes," ALEC continued, "he was always taking things apart and then having trouble putting them back together."

The three of us burst out laughing. Curtis's smile faded. "Hey, I told you I'd take care of it!" He said defensively. Then his voice dropped to a near-whisper. "Uh, ALEC, can you give me a hand?"

ALEC buzzed with joy. "You bet, Can-Man!" His screen filled with a complicated blueprint of wires and transistors. "Just activate my self-monitoring control system and ask for a diagnostic schematic of the heating system. I'll print out a detailed diagram of how to put all the pieces back together."

"I'm on it, ALEC." Curtis turned to reassure the rest of us. "Don't sweat it, Crew! I'll get the heating system going again."

"Thanks," Megan said sarcastically. "In the meantime, we're in the coldest region in North America in a giant metal box."

"Yes, and these metal walls can be a problem," ALEC said.

"Why do you say that, ALEC?" I asked.

"Metal is a very good conductor of heat."

"Conductor? You mean like in an orchestra?" I asked.

"No," ALEC replied. "Something that conducts heat well means that heat energy passes very quickly through it. So the heat from the warm air inside the train travels to the metal wall and then quickly passes to the outside of the train."

"Are you saying there's a problem with

the way the KC Express Train is designed?" Curtis wondered.

"No, but it was not intended for long-term cold weather missions. I'd suggest that, when we return to Kinetic City, we add some insulation, especially if you're planning any other cold weather expeditions."

"Insulation? You mean that puffy pink stuff they put in buildings?"

"That's right, Keisha!" A delighted "PING" sounded from ALEC, as if I had won a prize on a game show. "But that's not all!" ALEC's screens were immediately filled with photos of people in parkas, buildings under construction, lunchboxes and plastic coffee jugs. "Insulation is any material that slows the flow of heat from one area to another."

The monitor lights blinked and the hard drive purred with ALEC's next remarks. "Like I said, heat is a form of energy, and it travels. Heat wants to flow from warm areas to cold ones, but it can be stopped or slowed down by whatever material is between. Materials that make it hard for heat to move from a warmer place to a colder place are called insulators."

"Okay," I said. "So the train—and Arnold—need insulation. What do we use?"

"There is no perfect insulator," ALEC said thoughtfully, "but as long as you're trapping air so that it moves *with* you, you're going to be warm."

"What does air have to do with it?" Megan asked.

"It has everything to do with it, Megan," ALEC replied. "An insulating material alone doesn't keep you warm. It's the trapped air, heated up by your body, that does the trick. The key is keeping that warm air close to you, and not letting it be blown away and replaced by cold air."

Curtis nodded thoughtfully. "So, that's why we wear lots of clothes when it's cold, right?"

ALEC chimed in agreement. "Yes, but not just any old fabric insulates well. To be toasty warm, use fabrics that can trap lots of air, like wool for example."

Fernando looked confused. "Wait a minute . . ." He zipped open his parka and grabbed the bottom hem of the oversized, striped sweater he was wearing undeneath. "I'm wearing a wool sweater. Where's all the air getting trapped?"

From the side of ALEC's monitor, an arm shot out and held a microscope over Fernando's sweater. (If he wasn't used to those kinds of sudden moves from ALEC, it might've freaked Fernando out, but he took it in stride.) Within seconds, ALEC's monitor screens showed a magnified image of the wool fibers.

"If you look at a piece of that wool under a microscope," he began, "you see that almost eighty percent of that fabric is actually tiny air pockets between the fibers. That air traps heat and keeps it from escaping, creating a layer of warm air."

Fernando was impressed. "Cool—I mean, warm."

"But," ALEC continued, "when the wind kicks up, a loosely knit sweater like that isn't enough. Luckily, that parka you're wearing helps keep the cold wind from blowing through your sweater's wool fibers. That keeps the warm air in, even when it's blowing a gale outside."

"Thanks for the info, ALEC," Megan said. "We'll make sure we stay well-insulated—and Arnold, too."

ALEC purred happily. "And how is everything going with Arnold's movie career?"

"Not great," I answered. "That's why we came back to the train. Arnold needs some expert advice on dog sleds. Can you check your database for someone close by who knows about training dogs for that?"

ALEC hummed. "So you need the name of mushers?"

"Exactly," Fernando replied.

The humming increased in volume as ALEC whirred through his huge collection of files. Then there was a loud, pleased "DING!"

"Ah, you're in luck," He announced. "There's a champion dog sled racer right here in Fairbanks."

"Great," Fernando exclaimed. "Where is he?"

"You mean she," ALEC corrected him. "Her name is Musher Stewart. She's a three-time finalist in the Iditarod."

"Sounds perfect," Megan said. "Can you print out her address?"

Within seconds, a thin piece of paper tumbled out of ALEC's laser printer. "Tell her I said, 'Haw! Haw!'"

Curtis looked worried. "Something wrong with your sound card, ALEC?"

"No, but according to my online dictionary of native Alaskan slang, that's just mushers' talk for 'move on out!'"

Fernando smiled. "I knew that."

CHAPTER SEVEN

Meet Musher Stewart

To help Arnold with his mush team problem, we needed to find the local dog sled champion, Musher Stewart. ALEC's database said that her home was just a few miles outside of town. So we went to the KC Express Train's Garage Car and revved up the KC Snow Tracker. It's a big snowmobile, sort of like a golf cart on thick winter treads, that could carry four Crew members and, with a little squishing, Arnold, too.

We picked him up back at the film set, where he was talking to one of the clipboard-and-headset people about finding a new home for himself and the dogs. The film crew

woman, whose name was Katie, seemed
surprised to hear that we were going to
see Ms. Stewart . . .

"Strange lady, that Musher Stewart," the young production assistant said. "Don't tell her too much about the film, okay?"

"Why not?" Megan asked.

The assistant looked nervous. "I shouldn't have said anything. It's not like anything's been proven . . ."

"What? What are you saying?" Fernando's eyes lit up. "Is she behind the accidents?"

"Calm down, Nando," I warned. "I think you've seen one too many conspiracy movies. That's not what she said."

Katie shook her head quickly. "I didn't say it, but . . ." she lowered her voice and looked around to make sure no one else was listening. "Some people have wondered if maybe *she* cursed the film. She was one of the most vocal natives who spoke against the movie shooting here in Fairbanks."

"Really?" I tried to sound real casual, hoping I could get Katie to say more. "Did she threaten any kind of curse?"

"Oh, no, nothing like that," the assistant said. "She spoke out at a couple of town meetings, and then we saw her hanging around, watching us when we were out on location, but she's never done anything that I know of. Look, just forget it, please."

Katie obviously didn't want to say anything else on the topic, so we thanked her, and left. But now Arnold seemed very nervous. "Maybe we should not ask this Musher woman for help."

"Yeah, she could be dangerous," Fernando said.

"But we haven't even met her yet." I couldn't believe the Crew was so gullible. "Don't listen to silly rumors. Give the woman a chance."

"But she doesn't like the movie makers. Katie said so," Arnold whined.

"But Katie hasn't spoken to her personally," I reminded them. "Do we listen to hearsay or talk to her ourselves?"

Curtis stroked his chin. "ALEC said she's the leading expert on dog sled racing around here. That's what we want to ask her about, not movies."

Megan agreed. "And we don't have much time to track down somebody else . . ."

And so, we headed for Musher Stewart's home, about five miles outside of town. It was easy to spot the place—it was a beautifully arranged winter compound with a main house surrounded by a garden of ice sculptures and even a few wildflowers.

But the most amazing thing was next to the house—a large, glistening igloo that stood about twelve feet high! It was a dome-shaped construction, made entirely of blocks of ice, each about two feet high, three feet long, and one foot wide. It was the coolest little house I'd ever seen—and I don't mean that just 'cause it was made from ice.

Near the back of the place, we saw another fascinating sight—a team of nine sled dogs with shiny, thick fur. They were strapped in groups of two into a long leather harness, with one dog standing alone at the lead. The harness was attached to a simple sled of carved wood and oiled leather. The dogs pawed the snowy ground anxiously. I'm sure they would have run off with the sled except for a steel hook that was attached to the sled by a long rope and pushed into the snow to act as an anchor.

Arnold headed immediately for the dog sled and started patting the dogs and making goofy faces at them. We kept walking, closer to the igloo . . .

"Isn't this amazing?" I gushed to the other Crew members. "It's not just architecture, it's art."

Curtis wasn't buying it, but then what do you expect from a guy who thinks a house without video games is a home without civilization? "You've got to be kidding," he snickered. "I could never live in a place like that."

Megan was curious, but unsure. "It's just a big stack of ice blocks."

"C'mon! We gotta go inside." I turned back to call Arnold, but he was still patting the dogs. "Coming, Arnold?" I asked him.

"No, thank you. I want to stay with the big, shaggy doggies."

"Okay. But be careful there, Arnold," Fernando warned him. "Those dogs don't know you."

Arnold nodded. "I will be polite."

So we left him there and headed closer to explore the igloo. There was no doorbell. In fact, there wasn't even a door, just a low opening tunnel that led into the circular dome. We needed to go at least partway in to see if anyone was home.

We had to bend down to crawl through the tunnel. It was small and narrow—I guess so it could keep the wind from blowing in—and we had to take turns, single file, moving toward the large central room. When we came out of the tunnel, it took a minute to get our bearings. We were standing in the center of a circular room, made entirely of smooth, shiny blocks of hard-packed snow. Above us was a dome, marked with grid-like lines as light from outside crept in through the cracks between the blocks. It was beautiful, but strange too. Curtis shook, but it wasn't from the cold.

"Man, this place gives me the creeps. I feel like I'm trapped in a giant snowball."

"Ahem . . ." A noise behind us got our attention.

We spun around to see a dark-haired woman in a gorgeous tapestry-work parka. She must have come from the house and followed us in. "At the risk of sounding—shall I say, chilly—can you please explain what you're doing here?"

"Oh, hi!" Megan began. "We're looking for Musher Stewart."

"And you've found her," she said, not entirely happy about it. "That's me."

"Wow. I never met anyone who lived in an actual igloo before," Megan remarked.

The woman frowned. "Typical cheechako assumption."

"Cheechako?" Fernando repeated the word, smiling to himself at the sound of it. He glanced hopefully at the woman for an explanation.

"It's a native word for newcomers," she said, her scowl fading a bit under Fernando's curious gaze. "I don't actually live *here*," she replied, waving her hand to indicate the igloo, "nor do I eat seal blubber and ride my kayak out into the Arctic bay to harpoon whales."

"I didn't mean to be rude," Megan commented. "I've just never been in a real Eskimo igloo before."

The woman sighed. "I built this igloo as a personal tribute to original Inuit culture— that's the correct word, by the way, for the native people who settled these areas first."

"Wow." I was so busy being impressed by the igloo that I didn't mind the woman's sharp manner. "Are you an Esk . . . I mean, native Inuit?"

She nodded. "I'm one-quarter Inuit, on my father's side of the family."

"Cool," Fernando said. "I'm one quarter Native American! And I don't like it when people call me Indian, either."

Musher Stewart's eyebrows shot up and she chuckled to herself. She could see that we weren't out to hassle her. "Okay, so you kids have let yourselves in. You want to look around?"

"Sure! Cool!"

She seemed to appreciate the fact that we were really interested in her igloo. She stepped aside so we could move around a little and get a better look. I pointed to a beautiful carving of a woman riding in a kayak. "Did you make this?" I asked.

"No, but I collect native art," Musher explained.

"It's really beautiful," I said.

She looked like she relaxed a little when I said that. "The Inuit were skilled craftspeople. They carved stone, bone, ivory, and wood into things like cooking pots and good luck talismans." She sighed. "Too bad most of the beautiful work they do now is souvenirs for the tourist trade."

I looked at the rest of the Crew, holding back a smug smile. "I told you this place was a work of art."

Curtis still wasn't convinced. Without thinking, he blurted out, "It's still chilly."

Musher turned her stern eyes on him. "Did you expect a steam bath? It *is* an igloo, after all. But the temperature is a good fifty degrees warmer than outside. Blocks of ice are actually good insulating material."

Fernando chuckled. "Maybe we should show Arnold how to build an igloo," he said.

"Oh," the woman said. "Is that why you came to see me? Is someone you know thinking of building a home up here?"

"No, actually," I began, "we wanted to ask if . . ."

Suddenly, there was a howling sound from outside. The rest of the Crew and I exchanged worried looks. But Musher didn't seem concerned as she walked to a window. "Don't mind that. It's just the dogs. They get excited when I harness them for a run."

But when Musher looked outside, her quiet voice gave way to alarm. "Is that your friend out there?" she cried.

"Yeah," I said. "That's Arnold. What's wrong?"

We heard the dogs' yelping increase, and then a long "whooooaah" from Arnold. We rushed over to the window to see for ourselves.

"What does he think he's doing with my sled? Where is he going with my dogs?!"

Through the window, we saw the powerful mushing team dragging the sled away at high speed.

"You mean, where are your dogs going with him?" Megan yelled.

The large metal hook that acted as the sled's brake was no longer stuck in the ground. And Arnold, poor guy, must have been standing on the sled when the hook came loose, because now he was holding on for dear life as the sled flew away.

We all bolted for the tunnel and nearly smacked our heads against the low entrance (all except Musher, of course) as we raced outside to try and stop the runaway sled.

CHAPTER EIGHT

Doggone It!

We scrambled out of the igloo as fast as we could, but we were too late. The sled, with Arnold barely holding on, was already a hundred yards down the road. The dogs ran at full speed, howling happily while Arnold bounced wildly on the rear runner. As the sled disappeared around a bend in the trail, we could hear him yelling, "Where are the brakes?!"

We stood there for just a moment in shock. Musher disappeared behind the house, mumbling something about her snowmobile. Then Fernando jumped on the KC Snow Tracker. He shouted to the rest of us in a take-charge voice . . .

"Curtis, Megan, you guys stay behind. Maybe the dogs'll come back when they're tired or hungry." He pointed to the seat behind him on the Snow Tracker. "Keisha, c'mon with me. Arnold might need help."

There was no time to argue. Curtis ripped into his backpack and tossed me one of the Can-Do Communicators. I think he was glad to stay behind. Not that I was surprised—as I said, he's not much for the great outdoors.

I admit I was pretty nervous. With the crazed look in Fernando's eyes, I was afraid he'd suddenly decide he was a stunt man, too, and steer us off a cliff or something. But, I had a mission to accomplish, so I jumped onto the Tracker. "Sure you know what you're doing?" I asked as we zoomed off.

"Yeah, don't worry. My cousin in Blizzard Creek has a snowmobile. We used to race all the time!" I had no chance to second-guess him, or to turn back. Fernando gunned the engine and we burst forward, following the trail left by the dog sled.

I'll give Fernando credit—he knew how to push the Tracker to high speed and still maintain control, even when we hit some rough terrain that nearly bounced us off the machine. After a few minutes, my ears got used to the sound of the engine blasting and the wind racing by. That's when I realized there was another buzzing noise behind us.

I turned my head and saw Musher Stewart following about twenty yards behind on her own, smaller snowmobile. If looks could kill, Musher's face could have wiped out an army. She looked really mad. I wanted to catch up with Arnold as fast as possible, but at the same time, I was a little scared of facing Musher once we stopped.

About the time I decided the ride wasn't so bad, the dogs decided to take a detour off the beaten path. I guess they felt "the call of the wild," some primitive urge to head into rougher territory. Suddenly, we veered onto shrubby ground that had plenty of bumps. There were also lots of low-lying branches that nearly smacked us in the face as we sped by. It was hard to keep our eyes on the trail ahead, and on the sled we were chasing. Most of the time, unless the trail stretched out over a long straightaway, we couldn't even see Arnold and the dogs ahead of us. Talk about scary! We never knew what was behind the next curve. Every blind twist was a possible disaster.

We saw the sled take to a narrow road through a small grove of spruce. They were howling pretty fiercely, which should have told us something was up. Fernando revved the engine and followed. Then, just as we whipped around a blind corner, I saw a dark shape step into the trail ahead of us. A moose!

It was huge! Probably seven feet tall, with a giant rack of antlers that reached out at least four feet across. It stood like a brick wall right in the path of our roaring snowmobile. "Fernando!" I screamed. "Moose!" (Like he didn't know.)

There was no time to stop and nowhere else to steer. Unless we wanted to smack into a spruce tree instead, we were gonna hit the side of that moose like a freight train.

I closed my eyes and held my breath, thinking "What a bizarre way to go!" And then . . .

Nothing. No big crunch. No splat. Just the roar of the engine and the wind racing by. I opened my eyes and saw the trail ahead of us empty of everything except tracks made by the runners of the dog sled.

The huge animal had gone as suddenly as he arrived. Moose may look stupid, with that punching bag nose and those donkey-style ears, but this guy was no dummy. He obviously felt the same way I did about becoming road splat. In other words, he wasn't too keen on it. "See ya, Bullwinkle," I said to myself, and we were back on the chase.

But it wasn't like we could relax after that. The dog team was still going strong. We followed them across a river, speeding over an old metal bridge with only a foot-high railing on each side. It was narrow, too, with just enough room for the Tracker to pass. As we rumbled towards it, I saw a warning sign: "BRIDGE FREEZES BEFORE ROAD."

I thought of what ALEC had told us about insulation. I realized that the ground itself must be a kind of insulator. It keeps the underside of a road warmer than the top. Since there's no earth above or below a bridge to act as an insulator, it'll freeze sooner than the road that leads to it. Luckily, it wasn't icy that day. I hated to think how slippery that bridge would have been. If we had landed in the river beneath it, that would have been the end of us.

We raced along after the sled for almost an hour. The dogs were more powerful than we imagined. Later, Musher told us that a team of nine like hers, well-rested and well-fed, could go 30 miles per hour. To make things worse, they sometimes cut through narrow passages that our wider machine couldn't handle. Then we had to go around a different way and make up for lost time.

Finally, though, the dog sled took a wild turn and Arnold couldn't hold on any longer.

He flew off the sled runners and was chucked into a snowbank. The dogs kept running but they seemed like they were finally slowing down. Fernando and I rushed to the snowbank where Arnold landed to make sure he was okay.

At first, Arnold didn't move. He lay quietly, staring up at the sun, and smiled sheepishly. "Would you like to see me make a snow angel?" he asked meekly.

Fernando and I exchanged a knowing look and then each grabbed one of Arnold's arms. "C'mon, Nanook," Fernando said sarcastically. "Ready, Keisha? One, two, three . . . Heave!"

I took a deep breath and pulled. It took a few tries, but finally Arnold popped out, shaken but happy. He was grinning wildly.

"Ach! Thank you, Super Crew. I felt like the abdominable snowman!"

"Are you okay, Arnold?" I asked nervously. Maybe his crazy grin had to do with some kind of hypothermic reaction—a brain freeze or something.

Arnold grinned and nodded his head. "Yah! I am fine! That was some kind of wild doggie sled ride!"

While we were hauling Arnold out of the snow, Musher's snowmobile pulled up behind us. She whistled for the dogs, trying to get them to heel. It took her a while to get them calmed down, and then even longer to untangle their harness, which had bunched up when the sled flipped. But when she finally approached, she stared sternly at Arnold and waved an angry finger in his face. "You silly, dangerous man! That was a very foolish thing you did!"

I was all set to jump to Arnold's defense, but she continued. "I had that snowhook securely stuck in the ground. There was no way these dogs could have run off unless you loosened it!"

Arnold looked embarrassed, like he'd been caught with his hand stuck in the cookie jar. He tried to make nice with the annoyed woman. "You have some greatly pumped-up puppies there, Ms. Musher Stewart."

She smiled—just a bit—at the compliment and the excited way he delivered it. Arnold's such a big marshmallow it's hard to stay mad at him, even when he does something dumb. "Actually," she replied, "I'm amazed you held on as long as you did."

Arnold threw his arms up and flexed his beefy biceps. "Are you kidding? It was the best workout I've had in days. Better than the Abdominator."

Musher chuckled. (That was a first! I was surprised her face didn't crack.) "I'm glad you enjoyed yourself." Then she turned to Fernando and me and her face got stern again.

I put out my hand and smiled apologetically. "I know we've made a terrible first impression, Ms. Stewart, but please listen. I'm Keisha, and this is Fernando."

He stepped forward. "We're the Kinetic City Super Crew . . ."

The woman stared at us with new curiosity. "I've heard about you kids. You have that super train that you use to help people."

Phew! That was a relief. Sometimes being a Super Crew member comes in handy. Adults cut you a little slack when you're known for doing the occasional good deed.

"Yep, that's us," I told her. "We're here on a case. And we wanted to ask your help."

A small grin crept across the woman's face. "Okay. I can see we've got some serious talking to do. Let's get back to my home and warm up first."

"Ooh, that would be so nice," Arnold said.

The dogs had followed Musher to the spot, and now proceeded to pounce all over Arnold, showing him their affection. He enjoyed it with goofy pride. "The doggies like me, und I like the doggies," he told Musher eagerly. "They would be perfectly perfect in my movie stunt scene."

At the last remark, Musher's face went sour again. "Did you say movie?" she asked.

Arnold nodded. "Yah. I think so. Yah, I said movie."

Musher got all tense again. "Are you working on that film that's being shot around here?"

Arnold nodded again. "I am going to be *in* the movie." He paused. "I hope."

Musher was disappointed by the news. "That stupid movie . . ." she grumbled. "Those Hollywood types come up here and say they want to use this beautiful landscape, but they do a hundred things a day that go against native tradition . . ." she trailed off, annoyed. "Hollywood phonies."

I looked at Fernando nervously. How could we convince this woman to help Arnold with his stunt if she thought the movie itself was a bad idea? Suddenly, Nando flashed me a smile that said "leave it to me." He turned to Musher and turned on the charm.

"That's exactly why we came to see you. Arnold is supposed to do a mushing stunt in the movie, but the dogs they gave him aren't proper sled dogs."

Musher frowned. "Why am I not surprised?"

"We need the input of a local, someone who knows the right way to do things," Fernando was laying it on thick, but it was true. "Maybe if you spoke to the director, or John-Clod Van Dumm, you could tell him how you feel, get them to do things more accurately."

Musher stared back at Fernando, then at Arnold. "You could get me in to see them?" A little smile escaped from her stern face. "I must confess, John-Clod's movies may be dumb, but they *are* fun."

Arnold jumped in. "Yah, yah! I could introduce you. Und I could get you some hot chocolate, too!"

Who'd have thought—Musher Stewart, a Van Dumm fan. At least Fernando's little ploy worked.

"Okay, then," Musher agreed. "Here's the deal—you get those movie people to listen to my gripes, and you help me meet Mr. Van Dumm. Do that, and I'll let you borrow my mushing team. After I've taught you some basic mushing skills, that is."

Arnold was delighted. "Thank you. Oh, thank you so much!" he shouted, pumping the woman's hand so hard I thought he might pull her arm off.

I stepped in to stop him, but Musher broke away from Arnold's grip somehow and turned back to face Fernando and me. "I'll take the sled back. Keisha, think you can handle my snowmobile?"

I nodded. After watching Fernando negotiate that chase, I felt like I had the basics down pat.

"Fernando, you can give Arnold a lift on that machine of yours."

Fernando threw his hand up to slap Arnold a high five. But Arnold missed it and slapped himself in the knee.

Musher looked at the two guys and cast a knowing glance my way. "By the way, boys," she said with a motherly tone, "no detours and no racing! We've had enough wilderness adventure for one day."

I looked around us, realizing that I had no idea where we were. "Are we very far from home?" I asked.

"Actually, no," Musher replied. "These dogs have taken us the the long way around a fairly small area. If you follow me along the short cut, we can be home in twenty minutes!"

Relieved, I flipped open the Can-Do Communicator to give the good news to Curtis and Megan, back at Musher's igloo.

Fernando reached for the communicator. "Hey, can I do that?"

"Sure," I said, but I was a little confused. "If you really want to."

He pressed the send button and leaned in, lowering his voice. "Ice Base, this is Flying Snowbird, do you read me? Come in, Ice Base. We've caught the Wild Dog."

Curtis's voice crackled over the handset. "Ice Base? Flying What? Who is this? What are you talking about?"

"It's me, Curtis. Fernando." He lowered his voice again. "Mission accomplished. The eagle has landed. The credits are rolling."

I could just imagine Curtis on the other end of the line, shaking his head in dismay.

"Which means . . . ?"

Fernando let out a long sigh. "We've found Arnold. Everything's fine." Even from a few feet away, I could hear Curtis's groan through the communicator. "Man, Nando, why didn't you just say so?"

Fernando flipped the small device closed. "Oh well," he said. "Some people just have no flair for the dramatic."

CHAPTER NINE

Don't Sweat It!

Thanks to Musher Stewart, Arnold now had a dog sled team that was strong enough, and furry enough, to handle his big screen stunt debut. So much for Musher being the source of the curse. In fact, she was turning out to be the one thing that helped Arnold get his mind off the whole _idea_ of a curse. For the next two days, the champion musher gave Arnold a crash course in how to handle the dogs. And, after only a few actual crashes, Arnold took to the task like a pig to mud. He was also true to his word, and brought Musher to the movie set, where she actually became friends with the director and John-Clod Van Dumm. They were very impressed with her knowledge of native

Inuit customs and asked her to serve as a technical advisor on the film.

While Arnold trained, Curtis didn't move far from the KC Express Train. He said he wanted to test out his Trail Tagger and other cold weather gadgets, but we knew that he was working to make sure the heating system was in perfect shape. Otherwise, we'd never let him hear the end of it.

Fernando and Megan spent most of their time hanging out on the set, watching Van Dumm and Brock Hardley. As for me, I stayed close to Musher and Arnold so I could learn more about mushing.

For a short time, it seemed like everyone was happy and Arnold's stunt was in the bag. But it turned out there was one unhappy camper waiting in the wings . . .

"Brock! Brock! Is that really you?" Arnold was delighted to see the star stunt man driving up to Musher's compound on the morning before his big stunt. "It is my boss!" he shouted to

Musher and me as we worked to get the dogs in harness. "He has come to wish me luck!"

But Brock didn't look like he was in a helpful mood as he came toward us. He barely said hello, and just walked around the dog sled, studying the dogs carefully. When he finally looked at Musher, and she looked back at him, you could see that they didn't like each other much.

"Nice team," he said simply. "Professional?"

Musher stared back at Brock, unblinking. She nodded. "They're good dogs. They've won a few races."

Brock smiled, but it was a tight, nervous smile. He saw me studying him and switched quickly to his movie star grin. "Be nice to this woman, Keisha. Don't let her try any of her Eskimo voodoo on you."

Musher turned away, but not before I could see a fierce look on her face. If Arnold hadn't been there, I think she might have answered back with some really harsh words. Instead, she patted her lead dog and ignored the guy.

Brock, meanwhile, strode over to Arnold and put his arm around our friend's shoulder.

"I must say, you've been very lucky to find such warm friends in this cold territory." He squeezed Arnold's shoulder so hard I could see the strong man flinch. "Very, very lucky indeed."

"Uh, Brock, my shoulder . . ." Arnold winced as he addressed his boss. "You're hurting me . . ."

"Oh, so sorry," Brock said, but he took a moment to remove his hand. "I guess you won't be needing those dogs I got you anymore. Not when you've got this fine team."

"They may not be mush puppies, but they are still my doggie friends, Brock. I will take care of them until the film is finished. Please?"

"Sure, Arnold. Whatever you say. I gotta go." He spun around and walked off, as quickly as he came. I told myself to ask Fernando when he and Megan got back from the set if the stunt man was always this moody.

Later that day, Musher left Arnold with the dog team and went back to the set for a meeting with Hoppola about the proper way to build an ice fishing camp. Arnold wanted to try one more rehearsal, in full costume, and asked the Crew to meet him at the site of the stunt. So we all gathered at the strip of land at the edge of town where we saw Brock do his daring helicopter jump. When Arnold showed up, we saw just how much influence Musher was having on the production.

"Hey, look at Arnold's outfit!" Curtis exclaimed as the big man rode up on the dog sled.

Arnold was dressed just like an authentic Inuit! In his fur-trimmed parka and pants and dark, soft boots, he looked just like one of the pictures we saw in Musher's home of a native man going out on a hunt.

"What's with the spiffy outfit, Arnold?" I asked.

Arnold bowed. "Mr. Hoppola decided that my stunt would look better if I wore a costume like the people used to wear before other people came and became the people who lived here and wore other . . . uh . . . what were we talking about?"

"Your outfit, Arnold," said Fernando. "It's completely hype!"

"Thank you. I think," Arnold replied.

"Where'd you get it?" I asked. "It looks pretty authentic!"

"Brock asked a friend in the costume department to make it for me."

Fernando smiled at the rest of us. "What did I tell you? The man's just so cool!"

I was going to interrupt him right then to tell him about Brock's weird visit that morning, but Arnold was so happy, I didn't want to spoil things. He was turning slowly, modeling his new native wardrobe. "Musher has not yet seen my beautiful new costume. It will make my most excellent stunt look even more better. The costume lady made it for me from a nice, light, cotton material so I can run hard and fast without heavy weight."

I patted him on the arm. "You do look great, Arnold. Is everything else ready?"

He shook his head firmly. "Yah. The prop hand grenade is tucked into my imitation deerskin parka. The ladder is up, leading to the rooftop where I do my great jump. And, after I do my being chased, the doggies are ready to mash."

"You mean mush, Arnold," Curtis corrected him.

"Yah, dat, too." He put out his hand for all of us to shake. "Now you must wish me luck. I am going to chase myself around and jump to the doggie sled."

We gave him a quick cheer of encouragement: "Go for it, big guy!"

"Kowabangie!" With a shout, Arnold ran off.

The first part of Arnold's stunt consisted mostly of him running, since he was supposedly being chased. He looked a bit like a football player because he had to zig-zag at high speed, as if dodging bullets. When he reached a small shack at the edge of the town, he scrambled up onto the roof and then made a daring jump down, rolling across the snow and then leaping back to his feet to continue running.

All in all, he was looking very good, and we screamed our approval.

But then, as he turned and ran back, panting, toward the sled for the next part of the stunt, he slowed down. He seemed tired, although I know he had the stamina to do a lot more. And then he stopped dead in his tracks.

"What's going on?" I asked.

"I dunno," Curtis answered. "He's *supposed* to race the dogs down that trail and across the bridge."

But instead, Arnold flung his prop grenade to the ground and hung his head. He stood sadly staring down at his feet, barely moving.

"Arnold! What's wrong?" I called out. He just shook his head and waved his hand as if to shoo us away.

We all rushed over to see what could be making him stop the stunt so suddenly.

"What's wrong? What happened?" Megan cried out as we approached.

Arnold was nearly blubbering. "It's no use! I have reached for the stars and fallen on my buff buns." He sat down in the snow and wiped his nose, fighting back a sniffle.

Fernando patted him gently on the shoulder. "Don't be so hard on yourself, Arnold."

He shook his head sadly. "It's no use. With all that running, before I even get close to the doggie sled, I am freezing cold and damp from my manly sweat. I am so chilly, I cannot even lift a tissue to my runny nose. I am a frozen failure."

"No, Arnold!" Curtis said sharply. "Don't say that."

"Yes, Curtis! I say it because it is true. All I ever wanted to do was to use my beefy athletic powers so that I could become a media sensation like my idol . . ."

"John-Clod Van Dumm?" Fernando asked.

Arnold shook his head. "No. Tara Lapinksi."

"Well, you'll never get on the front of a soup can if you give up now," Megan warned him.

But it looked like that was exactly what he was doing. Arnold just sat there, glumly staring at his feet. He wiggled his toes and grimaced.

"Look—all this talk of staying warm, and still my toes are little popsicles."

He had traded his high-top sneakers for imitation mukluks—sealskin boots—but they looked all wet and soggy. I reached out to feel the material. It was thin—and very damp. "Arnold, what are those shoes made of, anyway?" I asked.

He looked at me like I was asking for the time signature of Bach's third cantata (in other words, like he had no idea what I was talking about). "I do not know. Does it matter?" he wailed. "I do not know what I am doing wrong, what I am *wearing* wrong to run and mush and be an Alaskan action hero." He put his head down on his knees and sighed.

I felt terrible. But as I looked around at the faces of the other Crew members, I could see that Arnold was the only person there who *wasn't* convinced that he could pull it off. We all had faith. We just had to convince Arnold.

"Arnold, my man!" Curtis said, grabbing his arm, and starting to pull him up. "This isn't like you. You're not a quitter."

"Yeah, Arnold," Megan cried out, jumping to Curtis's side and pulling on Arnold's arm, too. "You're an action hero!"

Fernando gave him a firm slap on the back that turned into a strong push up off the ground. "Up and at 'em, Arnold! You're a musher in the making!" he shouted.

It was like the Four Musketeers or something. I rushed over and grabbed Arnold's other arm. By this time, it wasn't really necessary. A grin crossed Arnold's face and he was using his own power to raise himself off the ground.

Soon he was standing—and smiling—again, and had that old Arnold spirit back. "Yah! I will do it again! I will do it again and again until I get it right." Then he paused. "But what am I going to do about my outfit?"

"Chuck it," I said. "That flimsy fabric is no better than the sweatsuit you were wearing when we got here. It's time to stop messing around and get you insulated."

"But, I've had all my shots," Arnold replied.

"No, Arnold, not vaccination—insulation." Curtis said. "Remember why you left that cold, cardboard house and moved into a house with insulation?"

"Oh yes. Now I understand," Arnold said. But he didn't really. A worried scowl came across his face. "But I cannot wear my warm, insulated house outside! I am not a turtle . . . I am a human being!"

"C'mon, Arnold! Think like an Inuit," Fernando encouraged him.

"I already think like an idiot—the director said so," Arnold said proudly.

"Not like an idiot—like an Inuit!" Megan joined in. "Fernando means you should adapt to your surroundings."

"Hang on, Arnold," I broke in. "I have an idea. You need to look like an Inuit, right? I think I have just the answer—as long as Musher doesn't mind." I turned to Fernando. "Do you know where she's meeting with Hoppola?"

"I think they're in the commissary," he replied. "We'll use the Snow Tracker."

"What should we do?" Megan asked.

"Take Arnold back to Musher's place and try to get him warmed up," I said. "We'll meet you back there. Come on, Nando, let's go!"

CHAPTER TEN

Musher's Sense of Snow

Fernando and I revved up the Snow Tracker and headed off to find Musher Stewart. Just as Fernando suspected, she was in the film crew cafeteria, sitting between Hoppola and Van Dumm. They were surrounded by a bunch of publicists, managers, and other hangers-on. The director and star were arguing over something. When we got closer, I realized it had something to do with whether Van Dumm looked better from the side or head-on for his close-ups. I tried not to think about the millions of dollars people got paid to make those kinds of decisions. Musher looked totally bored and frustrated by the whole thing. When *we finally got her attention, she gladly excused herself to talk.*

We explained the situation with Arnold's outfit and she agreed to come right back with us to help him out. We jumped on the Snow Tracker and rushed back to her compound. Arnold was standing outside the igloo, his hands wrapped around a steaming cup of cocoa.

When Musher saw him, she knew what the problem was right away . . .

"Arnold," she said with that familiar scowl of hers, "where did you get this pale imitation of a native costume?"

"From the wardrobe department," he answered, holding out his huge arms and swinging them so that the material swayed in the breeze. "You do not like it?"

Musher reached over and felt the material. "It's nothing but cheap cotton."

"But I look like an Eskimo, no?" Arnold asked, pained at her reaction.

"A real Inuit wouldn't be caught dead in an outfit made of fabric like that," Musher grumbled. "On second thought, maybe he would. Material that thin could kill you in weather like this."

"I have foiled again?" Arnold sighed.

Seeing his distress, Musher sighed. "Seriously, Arnold. You simply must learn about cold weather care."

Arnold's brow wrinkled, and he looked out at the sled dogs, who were still waiting for their chance to run. "I wish I was furry and warm like those mush puppies."

"Funny you should say that, Arnold," I said. "So, Musher, you think my idea will work?"

"I think it's perfect." Musher faced Arnold again. "Look, Arnold, if you want to look like a genuine Inuit—and keep warm, too—I have just the thing. It was actually Keisha's idea. Wait here, and I'll be right back with an action stunt man outfit that will have the costume department green with envy."

And with that, she hunched down and crawled through the tunnel entrance into her igloo. When she reappeared, she was holding what looked like a set of old rugs. But when she laid them out, we saw that they were genuine animal hides made into clothing.

Arnold groaned. "You want me to wear dead animals?"

Musher looked a bit wounded, and a little annoyed, too. "I realize that these days there's no need to kill animals for their fur," she began, "but this outfit belonged to my grandfather. He wore it back in the old days, when the native peoples hunted for survival. And they used every bit of their kill for food and for clothing. They even used the animal fat for oil to light their lamps."

Her voice dropped to a near-whisper. "I have kept these things in memory of my grandfather, and of the old ways." She turned to Arnold. "If you wear them proudly, they will keep you warm."

Arnold looked at the outfit curiously, and then smiled at Musher. He may not be the smartest guy when it comes to book knowledge—or common sense—but he's got more than enough heart. "It would be an honor," he said simply.

Musher smiled back. "Now let me show you how a real Inuit prepares for a run with the dogs," she said. "First, you have to take off that silly outfit."

Arnold smiled nervously. "May I use your igloo?"

Musher handed him the pair of pants. "Please do."

So Arnold squeezed his beefy frame through the tunnel entrance. She called in after him, "Put those on with the hair facing out, and pull the drawstring tight!"

A few moments passed, and then we heard Arnold's voice. "Ohhhh! These pants are soft as a baby's bottom!"

We all laughed. Musher said, "I'm glad you like them. The bearskin has been rubbed with oil to keep the leather nice and supple." She handed Fernando a few other items. "This is the inner parka," she said, pointing to a tunic-like shirt. "Tell Arnold to put this on, also with the hairy side out." Next, she handed him a pair of soft leather boots. "And these are seal-skin mukluks. He needs to tie these up around his calves, over the pants."

Fernando darted through the opening. A few more minutes passed, and then Arnold emerged. He looked great—rugged and cool, and very native.

"Do you like it?" he asked us.

"Excellent!" Curtis said. Megan and I nodded our agreement.

"Now, here is the finishing touch," Musher said, handing him a coat with a hood. "Wear this deerskin parka with the hair side in. And then these mittens . . ."

Arnold finished getting dressed. He had a huge grin on his face. "This is totally toasty."

"It gets better," Musher laughed. "Right now, some of the cool, outside air can still circulate around you, helping to prevent you from overheating."

"Yah, that is good. No sweat."

"Right," Musher agreed, "but when it comes time for your sled run, you need to make some adjustments . . ."

She reached forward and pulled the hood of the parka up over Arnold's face. She tightened the drawstring through the furry ruff and it came in close around his face.

"But if I wear the hood, I will not look so good in my close-up," he protested.

Musher stood firm. "Arnold, ninety percent of your body heat escapes from your head. If you don't wear a good hat or a tightly secured hood, you have no one to blame but yourself if you feel cold."

Arnold's face went all sentimental. "You remind me of my mommy," he said.

Megan let out a little snorting laugh. I poked her in the ribs and hoped Arnold hadn't heard her.

Musher tightened a waist cord on the parka and pulled the cuffs of the mittens up over the jacket's arms. "What do you think now, Arnold?"

"I don't feel the air moving around. Oooooh! I can feel it warming up inside."

Fernando gave him a thumbs-up. Megan and Curtis exchanged a high-five. "That's right, Arnold," I told him. "That's the air, trapped between the layers of clothing. You're insulated now."

Arnold slowly turned once more, modeling his newer, much improved, outfit. "I have just one question . . ." he began.

"Yes?" Musher replied.

"Will I still look like a movie star?"

We all shouted encouragement. "You'll be a regular Schwarzenegger," Fernando cried out.

Arnold stared at him, confused. "Who?"

CHAPTER ELEVEN

Between a Brock and a Hard Place

They say that clothes make the man, and that day I would have agreed. Inspired by his authentic Inuit outfit, Arnold was ready for some award-winning stunt man action. We hurried back to the stunt set and Arnold spent the rest of the afternoon rehearsing his running, jumping, and racing until he had the stunt down cold (hey, another pun!).

We stood with Musher and cheered for each and every rehearsal, happy to see our old friend doing so well. We were having such a good time, in fact, that we didn't notice someone else joining us on the *sidelines. Fernando was about to see for himself just how strange his idol had been acting . . .*

"Hello, Brock!" Arnold called out, pulling the dog sled up right next to us. "Look and see my new costume!"

We all turned to see the dashing stunt man staring at Arnold. He was smiling, but there was something about the smile I didn't like. It seemed phony, forced.

"Well, well, well . . ." he said. "That's quite an outfit you got there, Arnold."

"Is it not beautiful?" Arnold asked eagerly.

"Sure, but uh . . . what about the one I had made for you?" Brock replied, his eyes growing narrow and suspicious.

"Oh, Brock, thank you. That was very nice, too, but . . ." Arnold leaned forward and whispered, as if sharing a secret. "The material was too thin. I am sure the costume lady didn't know."

Brock nodded. "Right, sure. A mistake . . ." His smile tightened. "Well, I guess you're all set then for tomorrow, eh?"

Arnold's head bounced up and down. "I will make you proud, Brock. I will do a most excellent job. You will see."

"Sure, sure, Arnold." But Brock didn't sound very enthusiastic. "So, tell me again exactly what you plan to do."

Arnold was delighted to repeat it one more time. "First, I climb a ladder to the top of that cabin. Then I jump down to the ground and roll toward the doggie sled. Then I race the sled out to that small bridge that crosses the river . . ."

"That little bridge?" Brock asked, surprised but pleased. "Not much clearance there."

"That is what makes it exciting," Arnold boasted. "It is just wide enough for the doggies and me. And that is where I throw the grenade into the water."

"Right," Brock nodded. "But it's a prop, right?"

"Yah," Arnold replied. "There would be a big kaboom, but Mr. Hoppola doesn't want me to use a real grenade. You will see. It will be good, yah."

Brock seemed distracted. "Yes, we'll all see. Won't we?"

He took one more slow walk around the dog sled, but when he looked up and saw Musher glaring at him, he stopped. "Well, well, well, looks like you've got all the pieces together, Arnold. I guess it's time for me to . . . what's that you say, Fernando—'make like a deodorant and move on?'"

"Roll on, actually," Fernando said, and I could see that he was a little concerned by Brock's curt manner, too.

Brock bowed politely to Musher, nodded to the rest of us, and gave Arnold a wicked slap on the back that almost sent the poor guy flying into a snowbank. Then he walked off without another word. A moment later, we heard the engines of his snowmobile race angrily away.

I looked at the rest of the Crew, especially Fernando. He was confused. "Whoa, what was scratching *him*?"

Arnold looked at all of us, frightened. "Is there a problem?"

Musher walked to his side and gave him a reassuring smile. "Everything's fine, Arnold. You just worry about getting your stunt right."

But as he walked back to the sled and took off for one last ride, Musher came over to us. "I get a strange feeling from that man," she said.

"I know what you mean," Megan added. "He didn't seem happy at all that Arnold was finally on track."

"Yeah, and poor Arnold's worked so hard. Think of all the problems he's had," I said.

"Yeah, that chilly cardboard house," Curtis said, "those totally non-mushing dogs, that flimsy costume . . . Wait a minute!" Curtis's eyes were wide with excitement. "I just thought of something. What did all those things have in common?"

"They were all given to Arnold by the movie people," Fernando said.

"What a bunch of morons," Megan injected.

"Maybe not, Megan," Curtis replied. "What if they were given to Arnold on purpose?"

I could see where Curtis was going. "Yeah, by someone who wanted Arnold to be miserable, so he'd quit, or even worse, get hurt because he was too cold to do his stunt right."

Fernando looked confused. "What are you talking about . . . . oh, no!"

"Brock!" Megan exclaimed.

"But why would he want to mess Arnold up?" Fernando asked. "He's the only other stunt man around . . ."

"Exactly," Megan said. "Arnold's the only competition left."

We stopped for a few moments and thought it through. Then, like a cold wind, a shiver ran through all of us. Musher said quietly, "I think you've found your curse."

Fernando was having trouble giving up on his idol. "But Brock always acted so nice to me."

Megan turned to Fernando and said simply, "He's an actor. He can *act* nice."

"That's not what the critics said about his movies." I wanted to lighten up the situation with a joke, but Fernando was in no mood to laugh. "What about his foundation? He helps all those poor stunt men who get hurt on the job!"

Megan snapped her fingers. "That's it! That's the key!" She spun around on her heels and headed for the Snow Tracker. "You guys do what you can here to help Arnold. I've got to get back to the train."

"What's up, Megan?" I called after her.

"I'll be in the Library Car. I've got some research to do."

She ran off with a gleam in her eyes that told us she was on to something.

We turned our attention back to Arnold and spent the next half hour helping him finish his rehearsal. By the time Megan returned,

Arnold and Musher were busy feeding the dogs and getting them settled in for a good night's rest. But Curtis, Fernando, and I rushed to meet the Snow Tracker.

Megan jumped off the machine and raised her hands in the air like a victorious prizefighter. "I was right!" she announced grandly.

"About what? What did you find out?" Curtis, Fernando, and I had her surrounded.

"Well, when you mentioned that stunt man foundation, Fernando, I remembered an old article from the *National Tattler* that mentioned Brock . . ." she began.

"Okay, so you checked the database." Fernando was impatient. "What did you find?"

"Brock's foundation was investigated for fraud!" she told us.

"You're kidding," Curtis blurted out.

"No, look!" Megan pulled a printout from her pocket, unfolded it, and handed it to me. "It's all in here. I found it in the files, just a few years back, in the *Tattler*'s annual 'Slimy Scandals Report.' "

I glanced through it while she summed things up for the rest of the Crew.

"A bunch of stunt men who worked for Brock had some pretty serious accidents." She paused for dramatic effect. "*Suspicious* accidents."

"Wait a minute!" I interrupted. I waved the paper at Curtis and Fernando. "Remember—we're talking about the *National Tattler* here. Home of weekly Elvis sightings and three-headed alien babies. Don't you have any other sources of this story, Megan?"

"Of course," she groaned. "It was in *The L.A. Times*, too, but they didn't have any good photos, okay?"

Curtis let out a long, slow whistle. "Sounds like the real deal, then."

Poor Fernando was crushed. "Was Brock responsible? Did anyone prove anything?" he asked.

"No. There was talk of a big lawsuit against Brock, but the cases were all settled out of court. Word is, he paid them off to keep them quiet!"

"Let me guess," I said to Megan. "That's the Brock Foundation?"

Megan nodded. "You got it. It was just Brock paying the stunt people to keep quiet."

Fernando sighed. "So, Brock isn't really a nice guy who's trying to help Arnold get his foot in the door?"

"No," Megan replied. "In fact, I think he'd just as soon slam the door and break Arnold's toes!"

"I can't believe I fell for that snake's phony Hollywood act!" Fernando was angry at himself. "Let's nail the creep." He stomped off in the direction of the Snow Tracker. "I think I should go back to the set and see what Mr. Blow-Hardley is up to."

I followed him. "I'm with you, Fernando."

CHAPTER TWELVE

Bad News Brock

And so, Fernando and I went back to the film set to scope out what was up with Brock Hardley. Now that we knew what he was capable of doing, we had to make sure we kept an eye on everything having to do with Arnold's stunt. And while there's no crime in being a phony, if he was planning something new to mess up Arnold, we were going to put an end to it.

This time, I took the wheel on the Snow Tracker . . .

"I know you're mad, Fernando, but we have to lay low. If Brock has any plans to mess with

Arnold, we're gonna have to stay real cool to find out about it."

When we got to the film set, things were pretty quiet for the evening. Hoppola had gotten his shots for the day, and most of the crew was off in one of the recreation buildings, or having their meals.

But in one of the soundstage buildings, we found just what we were looking for. There was Brock, posing on the set—it looked like a fake mountaineer's camp—for the *Movie Times* photographer while the young reporter peppered him with questions. Thanks to a few well-placed props and camera cranes, we were able to sneak in pretty close to the scene without being noticed.

"Any advice for aspiring stunt men, Brock?" the writer asked, holding the recorder toward the burly bad guy.

"Stay out of the business, and let me do the tough stuff!" Brock replied with a chuckle. The reporter laughed, but knowing what we knew, his statement made my skin crawl.

"I know that things can get pretty dangerous in your line of work," the writer went on. "Have you ever genuinely feared for your life?"

"Are you kidding?" Brock hooted. "I live for the excitement, the drama, the adrenalin. What doesn't kill me just makes me stronger!"

Fernando and I exchanged a look. "What a crock," he whispered.

"What's this I hear about some kind of curse haunting the set?" the reporter continued. "Word is, you've had quite a few injuries."

"Hey," Brock responded, "I can't tell you everything's been smooth as silk, but those injuries wouldn't have happened if those stunt people had what it takes to do the job. The only curse around here has been the curse of amateurs doing a professional's job. I mean, look at me. I'm not hurt. That should tell you something."

"It tells me a whole lot!" I whispered to Fernando.

The reporter went on. "So who's this new guy testing out his stuff for Mr. Hoppola?" the reporter continued. "Do you think *he* has what it takes to do the job?"

Brock leaned over, shaking his head with concern, and placed his hand on the reporter's shoulder, as if delivering some terrible news. "I wouldn't pursue that angle, Andy," Brock advised him. "The guy's just not ready. Frankly, I think he's going to hurt himself bad. Real bad."

The reporter, meanwhile, wasn't so much worried as intrigued. "Hmmmmm . . . Maybe I should stick around and see how that goes . . ."

Brock's face flashed a look of pain. "You're not going to give that joker publicity, are you? I thought this story was about *me*!"

"Calm down, Brock, of course it is. You're the man getting photographed, aren't you?" The reporter waved frantically at the photographer, who quickly snapped a few more shots. "It's for a special edition: 'Where Are They Now? What Happened to Your Film Favorites of Yesterday.'"

"Film Favorites of Yesterday?!" Brock snarled. "That makes me sound like a has-been!"

"But Brock, you know how the business works . . ."

The stunt man smashed his fist against a fake pine tree, practically knocking it over. Flakes of plastic snow fell from the branches. "Yeah, I know how it works. Take a strong guy and bleed him dry, then find some new stunt stud and make him the action hero."

The reporter tried to make light of it. "What can I say, Brock? Everybody loves the angle of the fresh new face on the way up." He flipped the recorder off with a flourish. "And hey, if something goes wrong with the new guy's stunt, tragedy sells, too."

"Well, let's cross that bridge when we come to it." Brock looked down, and a sly grin crept across his face. "Maybe I should say, when *he* comes to it." At that, he laughed a short, cruel laugh.

The photographer and reporter looked at each other, confused. "What was that?" the reporter asked. "I don't get it."

Brock waved his hand. "Forget about it." He stood up and walked away. "No more pictures. I've got something important to do."

The reporter and photographer packed up their gear, muttering about Brock's moody attitude. While they were distracted, Fernando and I slipped outside to talk. We saw Brock head into the commissary, and watched through the window as he grabbed a tray and started dinner.

"I don't like the way Brock was talking, Fernando. I think he's definitely planning something else to make Arnold mess up."

"He'd better not try it while I'm around," Fernando hissed. I've never seen him so angry.

"He might have already done something," I said. "I think we need to go over every aspect of the stunt, every step of the route, just to make sure."

Fernando nodded. "Good idea. Operation Brock Watch is now in full effect."

The first place we checked was the cabin where Arnold was going to climb up a ladder and jump off the roof.

Fernando squinted at the ladder suspiciously, then pointed to a little pile of sawdust on the ground. "Keisha, look at this—sawdust." His eyes moved up and down the ladder and he stopped at the bottom rung. "Check it out. The ladder rungs are sawed part-way through."

Fernando put his foot on the bottom rung. "Look what happens when I try to step on this."

CRACK! The rung split right down the middle and Fernando's foot banged to the ground. Luckily, he was expecting it to happen, so he didn't have his full weight on the foot.

"If Arnold had done that with his full weight," I said, horrified, "he could have sprained his ankle, or broken his leg."

"Exactly." Fernando pointed to a building in the near distance. A sign over the door said "Prop Department."

I knew what he was thinking. "Let's find another ladder over there to replace it."

"We'd better hurry. It'll be dark soon." Fernando was right. Arnold's stunt was scheduled for the next morning and we couldn't do much once it got dark out on the trail.

We replaced the ladder, but found nothing else in the area. At least for now, we felt the place where Arnold had to do his chase scene was safe.

The only thing left to do was check the mushing route itself—about a quarter mile that led out from the town and over a bridge that crossed the Chena River. That's where Arnold would throw the grenade and then turn around to return home. That part would have to wait for daylight.

Meanwhile, we hurried back to tell Arnold our fears about Brock's sabotage. We met him at Musher's house, where he was finishing dinner with Megan and Curtis. Musher excused herself to work on some designs for the film and the rest of us gathered around the dining room table to discuss the situation.

But even after Megan, Curtis, Fernando, and I laid out all our suspicions, Arnold wouldn't admit that Brock was out to get him. "You have no proof. You have only circus-tential evidence," he said.

"You mean circumstantial, Arnold," Curtis corrected him.

"Either way, it does not prove anything."

"But Arnold," Megan tried, "I found a story in the newspapers about Brock's foundation . . ."

"Yah, he is a famous man, and his snow-shoes are hard to fill." Arnold was in his own world.

"No, you don't understand," Fernando pleaded. "Brock is gonna take you out."

"Yah, after the stunt. He will probably take me out for a nice brunch."

"Arnold!" I was really getting afraid for him. "We think the man is out to ruin you."

"Don't be silly." Arnold got up from the table. "I must go home now and get into my jammies. Tomorrow morning is a big day."

Nando and I followed him to the door, pleading with him to think about what we were saying, but he stood firm.

That's when Megan came up next to me and whispered, "Let him go. He needs a good night's rest. We can try to convince him again in the morning."

And so I reluctantly said goodnight to our friend.

Arnold probably slept like a log that night, dreaming of his show-biz debut. The rest of us didn't get much sleep, though. Funny how things had turned around. We came to Alaska to help Arnold get over his fear of a curse, but now here we were, afraid of something terrible happening, while Arnold snoozed away without a care in the world. Unfortunately, the next day we found out we were completely right to be scared.

CHAPTER THIRTEEN

Lights, Camera, Arnold!

The next morning, as Arnold ran around, doing last-minute preparations for his screen test, we tried to convince him that he could be in serious danger, but he wouldn't listen. He was determined to go through with his stunt.

So, while Curtis and Megan groomed the dogs, with Musher's guidance, and I double-checked all the wardrobe and accessories to make sure nothing had been tampered with, we sent Fernando out on the Snow Tracker to check the route one last time. What he found was a nasty surprise, something that would mean total disaster for Arnold and his precious "mush puppies" if he wasn't stopped...

A large crowd—many of the same people we had seen earlier on the film set—milled around, waiting to see the show. We noticed right away that Brock was standing in front, laughing with his pals on the crew. The reporter was there, too, and the photographer was scoping out angles to shoot from.

Then Cameron Martin Hoppola walked self-importantly onto the set, shouting into his cel phone.

". . . you call yourself an agent?!" He screamed into the receiver. "I coulda done 'Police Academy 12: the Donut Wars,' but noooo! You got me stuck in the world's biggest picnic cooler, freezing my buns off!" He paused, and noticed all the activity, as if he'd totally forgotten he was in charge of a multi-million dollar film production.

"Yeah, yeah, hold it a minute, Gary," he said impatiently into the phone. "Is it time for that stunt or isn't it?" he yelled to no one in particular, although a half-dozen head-set/clipboard types jumped to answer him.

I'd never seen Arnold look so nervous. He turned to us anxiously for support. "Mr. Hoppola looks so busy. And cranky."

"I hope we can stall a little longer," I said. "Fernando's not back from checking out the route. What if he found something wrong?"

"Time to rock and roll, Ruttabootie!" Hoppola shouted. "Let's get on with it, shall we?" So much for stalling.

Arnold wasn't about to argue. "Yes, sir. Haw Haw!"

Hoppola didn't get the reference. "Skip the laugh track. If we need one, we'll add it in post-production."

We gave Arnold some last high-fives as he took his place. Megan stepped forward with a clapboard. "Wow, I've always wanted to do this," she said. "Arnold Ruttebegger stunt man screen-test, take one!" She clapped the top bar down to meet the chalkboard, and the director yelled "Action!"

Arnold took off. The first part of the stunt went pretty smoothly. First he scurried up the ladder, then jumped off the rooftop, hitting the ground just long enough to spring through a big picture window into the saloon, spraying glass everywhere. (It was a special kind of glass that breaks into dull, rounded pellets instead of sharp shards.)

The crowd oohed and aahed. I slid over to where the director was standing and remarked casually, "He certainly can cover ground, dontcha think, Mr. Hoppola?"

He stroked his beard thoughtfully. "I haven't seen anybody move like that since someone put a jellyfish in David Hasselhoff's swim trunks."

Then Arnold burst out through another window and rolled into the street. He was on his feet in a flash as he made another daring leap, this time to the dog sled, and cracked the team into action. Curtis took a place next to Hoppola. "A perfect jump to the sled, don't you think?"

Hoppola was jaded, but impressed. "The boy has promise," he mumbled. Then he spoke into his cel phone. "Yeah, yeah, kiddo, don't get your boxers in a knot. I may have some new talent for ya . . ."

Arnold whipped around the crowd on the dog sled, and headed out for the old bridge. Things were going so well, we almost forgot about Brock Hardley. But as Arnold picked up speed across the field of snow, we saw Fernando coming the opposite way. When Nando passed Arnold, he waved frantically, but the strong man just waved back as if to say hello.

Fernando pulled up sharply at the edge of the crowd, leaving the Snow Tracker still running as he sped toward us. "We've got to stop him!"

Megan shook her head. "It's too late. You saw him—he's mushing like a madman."

"What did you find, Fernando?" I asked nervously.

"The bridge has been sprayed with water."

We looked at him, confused. "Water?" I asked.

"Remember—bridges freeze before the road does. There's no insulation above or below. That bridge is as slippery as polished glass. If Arnold tries to cross it, he could go right into the river!"

I stopped to picture the possibilities. "The sled could crash, the dogs could drown. Arnold could . . ." I couldn't finish the sentence. Arnold would be weighed down if that heavy outfit he was wearing got wet. And the river was deep, and wide, and freezing cold. It was too awful to think about.

"We've got to stop him!" I cried.

Fernando gave me a weird look. "Didn't I just say that?"

"Let's move!" Curtis exclaimed.

"But what can we do?!" Megan said.

"Wait a minute!" I turned to Curtis. "What about that Winter Wild Trail Whatever gadget of yours. You still got that?"

Curtis patted his backpack. "Sure, right here. But how can marking a trail save Arnold?"

Fernando gave me a quick thumb-up. "I know what you're thinking, Keisha. Did you fix it yet, Curtis?"

He frowned. "No, it still sprays gravel all over."

"Great! That gravel-spitter could give Arnold just the traction he needs to get across the bridge. Get on, Curtis. If we really move, we might be able to beat him there."

"But you drive like a crazy man," Curtis protested.

Megan and I pushed him forward. "It's your crazy invention. You're the only one who knows how to use it," I said firmly. "Just climb on and hold on tight!"

The Snow Tracker buzzed off in a spray of slush.

They told me later that, as they passed Arnold, they tried one last time to get him to stop, to wave him off the road, but he just smiled and leaned forward to urge his sled dogs faster. He thought they were trying to add more excitement to the chase by pretending to be bad guys.

The Snow Tracker beat the sled dogs to the bridge by only a few moments. Looking a little like John-Clod himself in high action mode, Curtis leapt off the back of the machine and aimed the Wild Wilderness Trail Tagger toward the bridge's roadway. CLICK! He pulled the trigger back. SPLOOOSH!! The thin gravel sprayed out like fine buckshot and scattered over the bridge. Thank goodness Curtis is such a lousy inventor.

He was barely able to scramble out of the way before Arnold and the dogs came flying past. He and Fernando held their breath, hoping the thin coating of gravel on the bridge would give the dogs steady footing on the slippery ice. They could see the dogs' paws scrambling as they first hit the surface of the bridge. But then, as they reached the layer of gravel on the surface, it provided some traction. The sled, too, wiggled a bit as it crossed, but Arnold was able to keep it under control.

Megan and I threw our arms up and

cheered. He was going to make it! Brock had really outdone himself with that frozen bridge mess, but the Super Crew had beaten him to the punch. Or so we thought.

Just before he got to the other side of the bridge, Arnold dramatically pulled the grenade out of his parka, ripped the pin out with his teeth and tossed it over the side. It landed in the river with a splash. The crowd waited, expectantly, but nothing happened. They turned to look at Hoppola, disappointed. He shrugged. "Look, I told him no explosives. He could barely handle the hot chocolate."

And then—KABOOOOOSH!

The river under the bridge erupted in an explosion of icy spray and fire. The whole crowd screamed in surprise and fear. The grenade had gone off!

What was going on? I had seen the prop grenade with my own eyes while Arnold rehearsed. Then it hit me: We hadn't checked it this morning. Arnold was all suited up when we got to the set. He had already tucked the grenade in his pocket. Brock had done everything to make sure Arnold's first stunt was his last.

The entire crew stood in shocked silence. I was about to go wrap my hands around Brock's thick neck when Megan shouted, "Look!" She pointed to the bridge.

The smoke and water spray had settled enough to see, and there was Arnold on one side of the river, and Nando and Curtis on the other. They were all waving. They were okay!

Everybody cheered and yelled like they'd all just won an Oscar. By the time Arnold had mushed back and skidded to a stop with Fernando and Curtis close behind, the applause was deafening. Then, through the cheering we heard a squeal of feedback, and a nasty crackle of static.

"Quiet! Quiet!!" It was Cameron Martin Hoppola and his megaphone. And he was hopping mad. "Rootabeelie, you pumpkin head! I told you to use a fake grenade!"

Arnold was stunned. "But Sir . . ."

"You could have been killed! I don't need that kind of publicity!"

"But Mr. Hoppola it *was* a fake grenade. Brock gave it . . ." Arnold stopped and his eyes went wide. He finally got it.

"What did you say, Rootabagel?" Hoppola demanded.

I stepped in. "He said Brock Hardley gave it to him."

The crowd burst into an excited murmur. They all turned to where Brock had been standing.

"He's gone!" Megan exclaimed.

Somehow, in the chaos of the explosion, Brock had slipped away—probably as soon as he realized his horrible plan hadn't worked.

"Find Brock Hardley!" Hoppola roared into his megaphone. Twenty different clipboard and headset types scattered like birds from a gunshot in search of Brock.

The *Movie Times* reporter was still there, though, scribbling furiously in his notepad. His

"Where Are They Now?" article had just taken on a new twist. Megan walked over and handed him printed copies of the articles about Brock's phony foundation. "I think you might want these."

Meanwhile, I ran up to congratulate Arnold. He gave me a big bear hug, patted the lead dog happily on its head, and then approached Hoppola nervously. "So, Mr. Hoppola, sir . . . Did you like my stunt? I mean, besides the part where I almost blew myself up?"

The director nodded coolly. "That wasn't bad, Ruttabegga. I think we can work something out . . ."

He was interrupted by the ring of the cel phone. He flipped it open and shouted into it, "Gary, kiddo, I'm a little on edge right now!" Then he paused. "What? They did? Oh, well, that's the breaks. See ya at Spago."

Hoppola clicked the cellular phone shut and picked up his megaphone to address the crowd. "Okay, everybody, pack it up and move it out! The picture's canceled."

"What?!" The crowd reacted with some confusion and disappointment, but being basically jaded show-biz types, they settled down soon. The excitement of Arnold's near-death experience faded as quickly as if a movie had ended and the closing credits were starting to scroll across the screen. The bustling crowd broke off into small groups and walked away, muttering to themselves.

But we all hung around Hoppola, concerned. Arnold was completely crushed. His massive shoulders slumped in defeat. "There goes my career," he moaned.

The director patted him on the shoulder. "Don't take it personal, big fellow. Guys in the corporate office decided they need something with lots of sunshine, babes and dudes in skimpy swimsuits. Happens all the time."

And with that, Hoppola spun on his heels and walked off toward his trailer. Arnold, desperate, shouted after him. "Wait! I can surf! I look good in a bathing suit. I am very pumped up. I love the Beach Boys! Wait! Wait!"

As Arnold trudged after the director, pleading and blubbering, Megan turned to us. "Boy, the Hollywood life sure is glamorous," she said.

Once we figured out she was kidding, we all had a really good laugh.

CHAPTER FOURTEEN

Arnold's Big Break: The Sequel

Poor Arnold. When we left Alaska, he was sitting outside Musher Stewart's igloo, drowning his sorrows in hot chocolate. We offered him a ride back to Kinetic City, but he said he needed a few extra days to say goodbye to his doggies. In our last Alaskan snapshot of him, you could see him standing outside the igloo, patting the dogs on their heads.

A few days later, we heard that Arnold had come home. Curtis was playing a video game on ALEC's super monitors when he decided to give Arnold a call and see how he was doing. He was just about to dial when Fernando came running into the Control Room . . .

"Forget the whales, forget sinking boats! Big budget blow-up movies are gone, kaput, yesterday's news. Besides, after our little adventure, I don't want to do anything that requires stunts." Fernando was wearing a baseball cap, backwards, of course, and carrying a copy of a book by Spike Lee. "I'm thinking of a small, personal film, an independent feature, something for the Sundance Film Festival."

Megan walked in right behind him. "It could work. It's a low-budget investment, but with the right press exposure, you can get back your money tenfold."

Curtis just smirked at the other two, but when he saw me right behind them, he practically pleaded, "Keisha, not you, too?"

I shrugged. "What can I say? Fernando said I could write the soundtrack!"

Curtis pointed to the KC Express Train's speaker phone. "Before you guys all move to L.A., do you have time for a little reality check? Let's see how Arnold's feeling after *his* show-biz experiences."

Fernando was game. "Good idea. Maybe he's made some new connections. Networking, that's the name of the game!"

Curtis sighed, and dialed the phone. He fed the call through the Control Car's speaker phones so we could all listen.

An answering machine picked up. "This is Arnold Ruttebegger talking on the machine, but not really talking to you right now because I am going away from the telephone as soon as I finish saying this. Please tell the beep your message."

"Oh, hi, Arnold. This is Curtis. When you get a chance . . ."

There was a click, and the machine cut off as the phone was picked up. It was Arnold. "Oh, Curtis! I am here. I could not get to the phone sooner. I am busy packing."

"Packing?" Curtis's eyebrows shot up at the news. He glanced at the rest of us.

"Where are you going, Arnold? Back to Alaska?" I shouted toward the receiver.

We could hear Arnold shiver over the phone. "No, no, no! Thank heavens. But John-

Clod Van Dumm liked my studly stunt and since Brock never came back . . ."

"What?" We were all surprised to hear it.

"They never found him?" Fernando asked.

"No," Arnold replied. "He left a note in his trailer that said something about leaving before he was asked to leave. He was always so polite."

I exchanged a quick look with Megan. Leave it to Arnold to always see the good in people, even when they didn't deserve it.

"But anyway, Mr. Van Dumm has asked me to work on his next film—'Beach Blanket Blow-Out!'"

We all gave a cheer. "That's great!" Fernando called out.

"Yah! I am going to the Caribbean to be Mr. Van Dumm's stunt double—and lemonade boy!" Arnold announced.

"Congratulations!" Curtis told him. "Let us know if we can help at all."

"Thank you, Crew," Arnold replied. "You are truly . . ." he stopped mid-sentence. Then he yelled, "Binky, no! Get down, you big bad doggie!"

"Binky?" I said. "Oh, no. Arnold, is that one of those bogus mushing dogs Brock gave you in Alaska?"

"Yah, it is!" Arnold replied. "I brought them all home with me to my now very tiny home."

"No way," Fernando exclaimed.

"Yes! You told me yourself they were not tough mushing-type doggies. I could not bear to leave them there. So, I asked Mr. Hoppola, and he gave me all nine of them for free! I am such a proud Poppa . . . Vincent! Do not chew on my mukluks!"

"So, Arnold," Curtis said. "I hate to ask, but if you're heading for the Caribbean, who's going to take care of all your dogs?"

"Well, Crew," Arnold said. "Since my doggies already know you, and you are such good friends to me, I was hoping maybe you could take care of them."

We all groaned. "That's what I was afraid of," Curtis said.

How could we say no to Arnold? We couldn't. And so, we became the Kinetic City Pooper Scooper Crew for a few weeks while Arnold chased his dreams of big screen fame. Oh well, as long as he thanks us in his Oscar speech!

THE END

Home Crew Hands On

Hey, Home Crew!

Being in Alaska, I kept thinking of my mom, and how she always yells out the door to me when I go outside in winter. "Take your mittens!" she says every time. Boy, am I glad I remembered her advice! I think my fingers would have frozen up there, and that's a sad thought for a musician like me.

I'm not joking, either. Frostbite can cause serious damage to your hands, toes, or nose—parts of your body that get colder quicker, because they stick out from the rest of your body.

I didn't know this when I was in Alaska, but your brain senses heat or cold because your skin contains receptors, which pass information about temperature to your nerves. There are separate receptors for hot and for cold.

Your brain takes the signals from these receptors and tells you if you're chilly or warm, but sometimes your senses can be fooled. (Think of optical illusions for example, when you trick your eyes into seeing something that isn't really there.) One way to fool your senses is to expose receptors to the same strong sensation for a long period of time.

Want to try it? Here's an experiment that'll fool your fingers!

What You'll Need:
three drinking glasses
one filled with hot (but not scalding) water
one filled with cold water
one filled with warm (not hot) water

What to Do:
Place the three glasses of water in a row, hot water on one side, cold on the other, and warm in the middle.

Put a finger from one hand in the hot water, and a finger from the other hand in the cold water.

Leave your fingers in the water for about one minute.

Now, quickly put both fingers in the warm water.

How does the water feel to your left finger, and to your right finger?

Now try this:

Take those two fingers out and put in a different finger, one from each hand.

Does the warm water feel different?

Here's what happened:

In this experiment, you tricked the temperature receptors on your fingers. The finger that was in the hot water was conditioned to sense heat, so when it's put in the warm water, this water feels cold by comparison. But the finger that was in the cold water was conditioned to sense coldness, so it registered the warm water as being hot by comparison.

Pretty cool, huh?

Your friend,
Keisha

P.S. Here's a cold weather tip:
Mittens keep your hands warmer than gloves
because your fingers can share heat!

GET REAL!!

During the Super Crew's "chilling" adventure in Alaska, they learned about staying warm in cold climates. It's no secret—insulation makes the difference.

Insulation is a part of our everyday lives, from the clothing we wear to the fiberglass material that keeps our houses warm. Insulating materials like wool sweaters or fiberglass wall filling are the materials that slow the flow of heat from one area to another.

Since heat can travel by way of moving airflow (that's called convection) or through solids (that's called conduction), a good insulating material is one that fights both methods of heat transfer.

Fiberglass is an excellent insulator for houses because it is made of thin, twisted fibers of glass. It takes a long time for heat to travel through all the tiny, intertwined fibers (think of it like travelling through a dense maze). The thickness of fiberglass also disrupts the flow of air, making it even harder for the heat to move through.

Layers of clothing work pretty much the same way to keep us warm. A windbreaker, for example, blocks the airflow. Sweaters, since they're made of fibers, put up a barrier that body heat has to make its way through as it tries to escape (think of a maze again!). And air itself acts as an insulation—the tiny pockets of air trapped in the fibers or between the layers of clothing help us stay extra warm.

Puzzle Pages

Chill Out and Stay Warm

Read what's in the shaded boxes to find out what does the job.

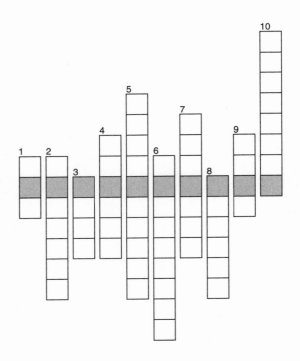

1. It's invisible and, when trapped between layers of clothing, keeps you warm.
2. Some use fur or feathers to keep warm.
3. This helps insulate Musher Stewart's house.
4. Some of the first people to build igloos.
5. Materials that make it hard for heat to move from one place to another.
6. The not-so-warm material used to build Arnold's first house in Alaska.
7. The material on the inside of the outfit Musher loaned Arnold.
8. Houses kept warm by ice and snow.
9. A good material often used to make sweaters.
10. Type of boots to keep Arnold's feet warm.

Answers on page 183.

Word Scramble

1. Arnold's feet were warm and toasty when he wore the (UKLUKSM) _ _ _ $\overline{}$ _ _ _
    5
   Musher Stewart gave him.

2. The original natives in Alaska wore clothing made from (ESALKSNI) _ _ $\overline{}$ _ _ _ _ $\overline{}$.
    1 3

3. Cameron Martin Hoppola was the (CRTEDORI) $\overline{}$ _ _ _ _ _ _ $\overline{}$ of John-Clod
    6 2
   Van Dumm's new action film.

4. Many people use the word (MOIKES) _ _ _ _ _ $\overline{}$, but the correct name for the
    4
   natives of Alaska is Inuit.

5. With a little practice and a good teacher, Arnold became an expert (SHUMER)
   _ $\overline{}$ $\overline{}$ _ _ _.
    9 7

6. Anyone living in cold areas has to be careful to avoid Hypo(EMRHTAI)

$\overline{}_{8}$ _ _ _ _ _ _.

Place the numbered letters in the spaces below to see Fernando's "high-concept pitch" about Arnold's Alaskan adventure.

Thanks to the Super Crew and Musher,

$\overline{}_1\ \overline{}_2\ \overline{}_3\ \overline{}_4\ \overline{}_5\ \overline{}_6$ performed his $\overline{}_7\ \overline{}_8\ \overline{}_9\ \overline{}_3\ \overline{}_8$

like a true movie _ _ _ _.
7 8 1 2

Answers on page 183 .

Mini Crossword

Animals that live in cold regions of the world have built-in insulation that helps them stay warm. Unlike humans, who need coats and sweaters to keep body heat from escaping, the animals—and plants, too—do it all by themselves.

Read the clues and fill in the missing letters of this mini-puzzle!

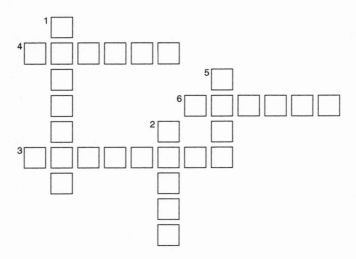

1. Wet fur would not make for good insulation, so water-dwellers like whales and seals rely on a thick, insulating layer of fat called _ _ _ _ _ _ _.

2. _ _ _ _ _ have the ability to put on large quantities of fat in the fall season which helps them stay warm as they hibernate through winter.

3. The air trapped between a bird's _ _ _ _ _ _ _ _ creates natural insulation to keep it warm.

4. The layer of snow on the ground in winter acts as an insulating blanket to keep _ _ _ _ _ _ warm.

5. & 6. A coat of furry hair that gets thicker in winter and sheds in summer keeps _ _ _ _ and _ _ _ _ _ _ at a comfortable body temperature all year round.

Answers on page 184.

Wrap It Up

Insulation keeps things warm, but it keeps things cold too! Make an insulated cup and see for yourself. All you need is two paper cups and some insulating materials such as paper, cardboard, plastic wrap, and cloth. Insulate one of the cups by gluing or taping the materials on the outside. Now, test it. Put an ice cube in the plain paper cup and one in the insulated cup. What happens?

Super Crew instant ideas
just add brain power and stir

Cool Crib

How does Musher Stewart's igloo stay together? Find out. Build an ice wall Musher Stewart Style—out of ice cubes. On a plate, stack the ice cubes on top of one another. Once your wall is up, put it in the freezer. Fifteen minutes later, take it out. What do you notice? If there's snow where you live, try making a life size igloo outside!

Answers

Chill Out and Stay Warm

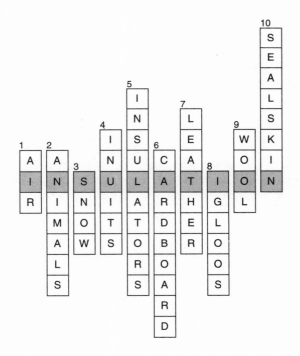

Word Scramble

1. Mukluks
2. Sealskin
3. Director
4. Eskimo
5. Musher
6. Thermia

Thanks to the Super Crew and Musher, Arnold performed his stunt like a true movie star.

Mini Crossword

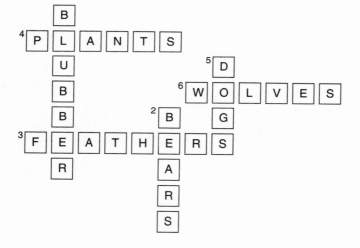

Other Case Files

From One Norse Town:
The Case of the Suspicious Scrolls

J. Angstrom Snerr had basically told the whole world we were going to show that the Kinetic City scrolls were fake. But we were a long way from any kind of real proof. Our only hope was that he had some real way to test out his theory, now that we had the chance to check out the scrolls ourselves.

We went to the Hushed Murmur Museum and knocked on the door to the small office that Trevor Ruse was using. He ushered us all in quickly. It seemed like he wanted to get this over with as soon as possible . . .

"Right. It's you. Come on in, then," he muttered, and shuffled toward the back of the room. "So, you want to test the scrolls yourselves, eh?"

"That's right!" Mr. Snerr piped up.

"If that's okay," I added, just so we wouldn't seem totally rude.

"Yes, yes, of course," Dr. Ruse replied. "I mean, I don't quite see *why* you need to test them. The museum's own testing was quite thorough, as you might imagine. And of course, normally we wouldn't just lend these out. But I've been made aware of your Crew's fine reputation, and if your seal of approval will help put these crazy accusations to rest . . ."—he looked up at Mr. Snerr when he said that— ". . . I'll happily entrust them to you for a bit."

"Thank you very much," Keisha said, putting on her best Official-Super-Crew-Business face. "I'm sure everything will be fine." Mr. Snerr looked like he was ready to make some kind of wisecrack, but luckily, PJ gave him a quick, gentle elbow to the ribcage before he could open his mouth.

"I'll go fish them out of the safe and get them ready for you to take along," Dr. Ruse continued. "I'll be back in a few minutes." With that, he turned and went into a doorway in the back of the room, and closed the door behind him.

"I think he's got something to hide!" Mr. Snerr whispered as soon as the door closed.

"I think we're wasting our time!" said PJ.

"I think I want a doughnut," said Max.

"What?" I asked him. He was staring off into the far corner of the room. I followed his gaze toward a half-full box of doughnuts on top of a tall bookshelf. Leave it to Max to find the only food in the room in less than two minutes.

"Max!" Keisha exclaimed. "Do you have to think of food right now?"

"Why not?" Max said matter-of-factly. "We're just sitting around." He had a point. "And I'm hungry." He walked over to the bookshelf.

"So what are you going to do with these scrolls, Mr. Snerr?" I asked him, leaving Max to his doughnut-hunting mission.

"I know just the person who can look at them. She can tell me exactly how old these scrolls really are."

"Who's that?" asked Keisha.

Before Mr. Snerr could answer, we heard a creaking from the back of the room, followed by a series of *thuds*. We turned around just in time to see Max jumping down from the bookshelf, splatting feet-first onto a chocolate éclair that had fallen from the box. Yellow custard oozed all over his left sneaker. The floor around him was littered with doughnuts and books from the now-half-empty bookshelf.

"Oops," Max said sheepishly.

"Max! What on earth were you doing?" Keisha scolded. She reminds me of my mom sometimes.

"I couldn't reach the doughnuts, so I tried climbing up the bookshelf," Max replied, scraping custard from his treads with a square of wax paper from the doughnut box.

"Well, don't just stand there," she said. "Pick that stuff up before Dr. Ruse comes back!"

I trotted over to help Max. When I picked up a thick textbook called *Medieval Norse History*, I saw something that caught me completely off guard. The book had fallen open, face-down, and when I lifted it up, there was a small pile of money underneath it. And we're not talking spare change— we're talking bunches of crisp one-hundred dollar bills!

What's more, a couple other bunches of bills fell out of the book when I picked it up. I turned the book over and saw that someone had carved a big hole in all of the pages, leaving a space to stash the cash. I had no idea what the money was for, but it looked like Max's stomach had led us to our first clue.

"Hey, Crew," I said, trying not to speak too loudly. "Get over here *now*! Look at what's in this book!" I showed them the carved-out pages and the wads of hundreds.

"Jumpin' Jehosaphat!" Mr. Snerr yelped. We had to *shush* him back down to a whisper.

"There must be ten or twenty thousand dollars here!" said PJ, flipping through the bills with amazement.

"*Now* tell me there's nothing sneaky going on!" Mr. Snerr said triumphantly.

He was right. Up until now, everything had looked pretty normal on the museum's end. But how could we explain *this*?

⇒◆⇐

From Rock the House:
The Case of the Meteorite Menace

"Whoa!" Megan yelled. "We've been hit!!"

Bang! Another one.

"What is going on!?" Megan yelled again. "It's like those meteorites are aiming for us!"

It was bizarre alright, but I wasn't worried about getting hurt. The X-100's roof has triple-reinforced titanium plates. There was no way those falling rocks could get to us. At least until Max leaped to our rescue.

"I'll activate the force field!!" he screamed out, lurching for the Control Panel.

"Max!!" I yelled, trying to stop him. "We don't even have a force field." Too late. He flipped one of the switches closest to ALEC's keyboard. The result was immediate. A big section of the ceiling slid open. The train's PA system came on to announce what was up.

"Activating sun roof now," it said in its cold, robotic voice. "Enjoy the sunshine!"

"Uh oh," Max said.

"Uh oh" was right. I looked up. I could see the black of the night and feel the tiny drops of drizzle hitting my face.

"Close it, Max!" Megan screamed. "Now!"

Too late. The thing we all most feared finally happened. There was an ear-splitting bang as a meteorite fell into the Control Car! The rock had caught the side of the control panel, missing Max by less than four feet. Max was fine, but the impact had activated one of the control panel switches.

"Activating thruster rockets now," the trains voice announced.

"Oh no!" I said. The thruster rockets were supposed to be used only for traveling across empty places like the Sahara desert or the Utah salt flats. We were halfway up a wooded hill with the lights of Kinetic City spread out below us! I didn't even want to think about the damage we would cause if we went barreling out of control.

"Fire up ALEC for the override!" I shouted.

"Check!" Keisha said, reaching for the keyboard and typing like mad.

I could hear the thruster rockets moving into place along the sides of the train. In a few seconds, they'd fire up and send the entire KC Express shooting off toward down-town like a giant missile.

"Heelllooo, Crew," ALEC came on as chipper as ever. "Did you know that over 16,000 meteorites have been collected from Antarctica? Because of the conditions there, the space rocks are relatively easy to find, often lying on the surface of the ice."

"Override the thruster rockets, ALEC!" Keisha wisely called out as loud as she could.

"The thruster rockets have been activated?" our computer asked with a few, surprised sounding beeps. "They should never be turned on in a populated . . ."

WWWHHHOOOSSSHHH!!!

The rockets fired. The sudden acceleration knocked all four of us back against the Control Car door. I don't know if you've ever seen a drag race, but the KC Express Train would've left any dragster choking in our dust. To make matters even worse, the roof was still wide open. Cold, wet air blew in our faces as we tore down the side of the hill like some kind of wild roller-coaster ride of no return.

"Make it stop, ALEC!" Max screamed.

"What?" the computer asked calmly. "The thruster rockets?"

"Yes!!" we all yelled. Like I say, you have to be specific with ALEC. He may have every fact in the world in his database, but he doesn't have a byte of common sense.

I looked out the Control Car window. The lights of

Kinetic City had grown noticeably brighter. No wonder. We were speeding across fields and racing toward town at over three hundred miles an hour! All that stood between us and smashing into a shopping mall was one last cornfield. Still pressed against the Control Car door, there was nothing any of us could do to prepare for impact.

———⬖⬗⬖———

From This School Stinks:
The Case of the Secret Scent

When we last left Brian and his friends, we kind of
left them with something dangerous: a taste for
revenge on Snurdburg. I had figured it was all talk—
after all, if there's one thing Brian's good at, it's
talk. But judging from what Principal Marsh told us
he overheard, it sounded like Snurdburg was in for a
payback that they didn't even deserve.

We rushed straight down to the cafeteria,
hoping to catch them before they did anything really
nasty. I hoped we weren't too late. The last thing
we needed was for the Super Crew to be responsible
for some kind of prank war. When we first opened the
cafeteria doors, though, it looked like they were
gone. The whole lunchroom was deserted.   There was
only one sign of life . . .

"Ugh!" PJ said, as soon as she took a step inside the
lunchroom. "Do you smell that?"

I sure did. Believe me, the only way you could miss it
is if you had a world-class cold or a bargain-basement nose
job. It was one of the grossest things that's ever gone in or

out of my nostrils, if you get my drift.

"It's worse than that dead squirrel in our chimney!" Keisha said, holding her nose.

"Where the heck is it coming from?" Fernando asked.

I stepped around the room. The closer I got to the kitchen, the worse it got. "I think it's in there!" I said, pointing to the kitchen door. Then suddenly, a loud whirring sound, like from a blender or some kind of machine, came from behind the door.

"Someone's in there!" Keisha said.

"Maybe it's them! Let's go in!" said PJ.

We walked slowly up to the kitchen door—we kind of had to get used to the smell bit by bit. Finally, we knocked. "Brian? You in there?" I yelled. No answer. The machine noise had to be drowning me out anyway. I signaled to the rest of the Crew to follow me, and swung the door open.

There he was, all right. I saw Brian, all of his band mates, his friend Chad from the basketball team, a couple other guys in basketball jerseys, and even that girl Gwen from the debate team. They were standing around an industrial-size mixing bowl, blending together a disgusting green sludge in the electric mixer. The counters were covered with buckets full of some unrecognizable glop. And the smell was ten times worse.

NOW HEAR THIS!!

Every week tune in to the Kinetic City Super Crew radio show!

If you think reading about the Crew is cool,
wait till you hear them blasting out of your radio.
Every week the Super Crew find themselves tangled up
in danger and mystery in a different place...
from the icy tundras of Alaska to the busy
streets of Kinetic City.

Call 1-800-877-CREW (2739)

to find out where you can tune in to hear
the next awesome episode of
Kinetic City Super Crew.

KCSC is featured on Aahs World Radio and finer public radio stations around the country.

 AMERICAN ASSOCIATION FOR THE ADVANCEMENT OF SCIENCE   National Science Foundation

How would you like to try solving your own mystery with the Super Crew? It's waiting for you now, at Kineticcity.com!

You'll also find games, info on your favorite Super Crew members, online chats, and cool things to download, like stationery and screen savers. There's even a page for teachers and parents.

When you get to the site make sure you bookmark it. You'll want to go there every day because there's always something new and fun happening at Kinetic City Cyber Club!

AMERICAN ASSOCIATION FOR THE ADVANCEMENT OF SCIENCE

National Science Foundation

The staff of the Kinetic City Super Crew Radio Project:

Executive Producer:	Bob Hirshon
Senior Producer:	Joe Shepherd
Producer/Engineer:	Barnaby Bristol
Assistant Producer:	Anna Ewald
Director:	Susan Keady
Writers:	Chuck Harwood
	Marianne Meyer
	Sara St. Antoine
	Justin Warner
Associate Editor:	Samantha Beres
The Crew:	Damion Connor
	Elana Eisen-Markowitz
	Joaquin Foster-Gross
	Reggie Harris
	Melody Johnson
	Monique McClung
	Jennifer Roberts
	Paul Simon
Business Manager:	Thu Vu
Outreach Coordinator:	Corette Jones
Project Assistant:	Renee Stockdale-Homick
Cyber Club Producer:	Kimberly Amaral
EHR, Head:	Shirley Malcom
Director,	
Public Understanding of Science:	Alan McGowan
Science Content Advisor:	David Lindley
Executive Officer, AAAS:	Richard Nicholson